THE SHOT

This book is a work of fiction. All characters, places, and events in this novel are fictitious and a product of the author's imagination. Any resemblance to actual events or locales or persons, living or dead, is entirely coincidental.

Author: Doctor Gaines

Cover illustration: Ryan Richmond
www.ryanrichmond-art.com

Cover design: Emmy & Doctor Gaines
www.searchingforthelight.com

Published in the USA by Muzzleland Press, 2015. First edition.

ISBN-10: 0989924025

ISBN-13: 978-0-9899240-2-3

THE SHOT

DOCTOR GAINES

MUZZLELAND PRESS © MMXV

SEVEN

It is Year Five, and things have progressed to the point that I am forced to live in a state of almost constant hiding from the users.

My apartment sits on the third floor of a long abandoned building with no power, no light, no water, no heat. It is a dark and dingy space with nothing in it but a mold-smelling couch, an old mattress on the floor and a smattering of lamps, appliances, and other things that require electricity which are now rendered useless. It would be too much trouble, and more importantly, too risky, to haul these items down three flights of stairs to a Dumpster outside that never gets emptied anymore, so I just leave them to collect dust and remind me of the conveniences that I once had. I chose the apartment because of its largely isolated location in town and for its plain, unnoticeable quality; the sort of structure that blends into the bland grey landscape of similar architecture. However, I have been forced to relocate several times over the years, and almost surely will again.

It was not always this way, even in the first few years of The Shot. There was a time when I could still go out in the open with relative ease to scavenge the grocery stores for bottled water or food that had not yet expired, and the users would pretty much leave me to my business if I looked and sounded like one of them. But they have gotten smarter, more observant, and more *insistent*. They have made it too dangerous to be out in the open, so now I go out only when absolutely necessary.

On the rare occasions that I do go outside, I have to put on an act in order to blend in. One wrong move in front of the users—failure to rave about the glories of The Mothership, coming up short on quoting a piece of Scripture, or betraying even the smallest hint that I am not high on The Shot at all times like they are—could land me with a syringe to the gut and a six hour hallucination that I would rather die than endure. And as someone who has never taken The Shot before, there's the horrifying prospect of becoming hooked from the first use, as has happened with so many others.

I say that the users have become more insistent because they used to just offer The Shot to those who did not partake of the drug. Now they skip the asking part and plug you with a needle before you can breathe a word of protest.

With stakes like that, it's easier to just stay indoors.

In the early days, The Shot had just seemed like a trend. Something that might rise up into brief sub-cultural popularity, reach a peak, and then recede out of the spotlight to give way to the next new substance people were raving about. It was the sort of thing you might hear about being passed around at a party, or referenced in the headline of some off-color tabloid. It was something niche-y and hip for celebrities to offhandedly confess to using, usually on late night talk show interviews, always admitting this with a smirk and a glint in their eye, self-impressed by just how very *naughty* they were being. The online community treated it like a joke, as it was perceived to be in the realm of extreme and damaging narcotics like crack or meth that a "regular" upstanding citizen would never consider using. Word was that The Shot made a person talk about the Bible and outer space concurrently, as if those two things were inseparably connected, which only added to the fodder for making fun of the substance.

People would tweet John 3:16 or other Scripture references, then add, "I am SO high right now #TheShot." Memes were made by taking screenshots of charismatic TV preachers, quoting something particularly outlandish that they had said at the top of the image, then at the bottom (always in Impact font, true to meme form) would be: **HIGH, I'm "HI" on THE SHOT.** There was even an entire sub-reddit devoted to such images, reddit.com/r/ImOnTheShot.

So much for social media sites now, all of those big colorful companies that they used to say would never die, that were supposed to be a permanent installation to our cultural experience. Try to log on to one of those now and you will find a tangled, glitchy, skeletal mess of pixels and broken pages; the last remnants of ones and zeroes representing what the web once was that have somehow not crumbled into digitized nothingness. Who would have thought that the world's most powerful tool would one day fade out of our culture into complete obscurity and uselessness? If there is one thing you are guaranteed *not* to encounter these days, it's a face pointed downward, distracted by the black mirror of a mobile screen. In another time and place I would have probably considered that a *positive* thing for our species. It's only that what humans are currently interested in is immeasurably worse.

"Taste, brothers! See, sisters!" users of The Shot would say in the early days, shouting in the streets to anyone walking past. "The world spins on in disbelief and even so, The Mothership approaches! Will you, too, partake of the gift and eagerly await Her arrival?" It became a normal part of life, seeing users around, babbling half-Scriptures and talking about outer space. "Regular" people ignored them at first, although if any other users happened to be passing by they would join in with the shouters in hearty agreement, making a scene until the police came along and broke them up.

That, or you'd see someone huddled near a window at a coffee shop or in a pub, gazing out with their face pressed against the glass and saying things like "My God, *the stars!* Do you see them?"—this being in the middle of the day and with full sunlight—"So *close*, as if we could reach out and grab them! Oh, how I long to meet Her in the skies..."

Despite the public's initial reaction to the substance, within three years of The Shot's first known appearance in Southern California (which is undocumented and based solely on rumor), large scale surveys by Gallup and a handful of universities found that the majority populations of North America and Europe were openly—and wholeheartedly— using The Shot. Most individuals admitted to taking doses multiple times a day. By then, it could hardly be considered a niche drug anymore with statistics like that.

Only two years later, nearly everyone on the planet was taking The Shot. There were not any studies or surveys to confirm this. You could see the truth of it as plain as day when you stepped out your front door, when you looked people in the eyes, when you heard the insane things rolling off of everyone's tongues.

I say *nearly* everyone on the planet because I am one of the few holdouts—or perhaps the *only* holdout. There may be a handful of others like me scattered around, but if there are, we have not crossed paths. For the most part, my life consists of staying indoors, and when I'm outdoors, trying to hide the fact that I am not a user by acting and appearing like one of them. If they catch on to me, the results will not be pretty.

The Drug Enforcement Administration (when it still existed) refused, even after months of extensive testing and

clinical research, to classify The Shot as a Schedule I drug—
even though it most definitely and undoubtedly ought to
be for its hallucinogenic and addictive qualities. The DEA
claimed that their researchers—a handful of bozos in white
labcoats, no doubt—could not identify all of The Shot's
properties, and that they would need more time for further
testing. What they did know was that The Shot's chemical
makeup is, on paper, incredibly rudimentary—a simple
substance of only four or five discernible "ingredients."
However, the elements it contains are unrecognizable and
incomparable to any other drug encountered before. Their
reports were littered with terms like "unidentified" and
"undefined."

One phrase in particular was quickly snatched up by
the media groups and replayed ad nauseam as a soundbite:
"While studies thus far are inconclusive, current evidence
suggests that The Shot is not harmful for consumption."

For many, the matter was settled right then and there.
It also threw up an enormous red flag (for me, anyway) that
something extremely suspicious was happening behind the
scenes. The DEA was hardly known for such negligence
and flippancy when it came to classifying a substance. They
would not lightly spend millions of tax-payers' dollars and
thousands of hours researching something only to come out
and say, "We're not sure about this stuff, but it's probably no
big deal." It is possible that there was governmental pressure
behind these ambiguous statements (although for what
purpose, I cannot imagine), but I think the truthful answer
is probably much simpler: the boys at the DEA were already
using The Shot themselves.

This all happened about two years after the emergence
of The Shot on the streets, at which time it had already laid
claim on millions of regular users and was a much-debated

topic of heated discussion. There was a period of time when it was literally all you would hear about on the political talk shows from the left, the right, and the in-between. The big news channels verbally banged down the doors of the White House, hollering for them to give an official position on the substance, but no statement ever came. When it came to The Shot, the Oval Office turned a deaf ear—another red flag.

The local news stations would feature interviews recorded with citizens around town, asking people their personal opinions on the moral implications of using the drug. Most of them were all for it. TV preachers spat and gleamed with sweat and grew red in the face screaming about the eternal consequences of using The Shot, how the syringes people were shooting themselves up with were keys to the very gates of Hell. The green gook that the heretics were forcing into their bodies was a gift from The Devil himself. There were advocates who gathered on street corners with homemade cardboard signs (featuring tall letters written in bold green, naturally) that read things like "DONT TAKE THE 1ST GOOD THING TO HAPPEN TO ME!" or, "THE SHOT IS A GIFT TO MANKIND" and even, "DON'T KNOCK IT TIL YOUVE TRIED IT! ☺ "

Meanwhile, The Shot remained "Unclassified" as a substance and the "further testing" by the DEA never happened, probably because their guys were so damn busy getting high on the stuff that they just hoped nobody would ask questions. People *did* ask questions at first, but those who did were ignored by the parties in charge. Eventually, even the drug's harshest critics dropped their protests and moved on. And by moved on, I mean they started using.

At this point, five and a half years or so since The Shot cropped up from out of nowhere—and I do mean literally out of *nowhere*—no one is asking questions anymore. No one is interested in studying The Shot, its effects, or its probable health-damaging implications. Everybody is too busy using.

I remember when people started using it at work, at the newspaper. I had six years of experience under my belt at the time, having started out as a lowly copy editor straight out of college (with a shiny new degree in Journalism in my back pocket that had counted for just about nothing when it came to real world employment). I was paying my dues, working up through the ranks, doing whatever other tired career tropes apply, with my eye on being either a full time columnist or a beat reporter. I had even convinced the Managing Editor to take a look at a few of my one-off pieces, three of which were printed in obscure, deeply-buried sections of the paper. But it was still progress, for which I was pleased. I would take whatever I could get.

It had seemed like I was gaining traction until one day the Editor-in-Chief came into the office, a towering, short-tempered Jewish man with a large gut named Barry Weitzmann. He was high as a kite and had a big sunny smile on his face—a rare sight if ever there was one. He began shouting across the newsroom that he had something wonderful to tell us. He made sure the entire staff was gathered—thirty-seven people in all, including journalists, editors, graphic designers, the whole lot—before he went on a nonsensical rant about a ship and salvation and how much he wanted us all to taste and to see this thing called "The Shot."

I and much of the other staff looked around at each other bewildered, wondering if there was going to be a big punchline at the end of this speech (even though Barry was hardly one for joking). But no punchline ever came. Some of the staff even appeared to be quite engaged in what he was saying.

Weitzmann finished his address, still cheery as could be, with the recommendation that we try The Shot for ourselves, that he could personally guarantee we would not regret it. In fact, he said, to *not* try it would be robbing ourselves of a wonderful experience. With that, he told everyone to have a great day and proceeded to step into his glass-walled office and kick back in his reclining desk chair. He put his feet up on his desk, folded his hands behind his head, and stared out the window with a big grin for the rest of the day.

The next morning, Weitzmann did not come back into work, nor did our Managing Editor. They did not return for the rest of the week, and our assistant editors had to make all of the final decisions for what went to print, a task for which they were hardly prepared.

The following week, our Sports staff stopped showing up, along with a few of the photo editors. The week after that, we were down to two-thirds of a full staff, and the material we were putting out was slapped together and surely riddled with copy errors and unverified information.

A month passed since any of us had seen Weitzmann or the Managing Editor, and we were down to putting out one paper a week instead of the usual five. If our reading public had noticed, we hadn't heard about it. There were about nineteen of us still coming in to the office on a daily basis, but half of that number spent the day staring out the window and muttering about stars or whispering pieces of Bible verses. The "work" they turned in was nothing but spaceship doodles and gibberish. The newsroom itself was messy and neglected.

Seven weeks after Weitzmann's speech in the newsroom, I stopped receiving paychecks that were set up to automatically deposit into my checking account. It was not a surprise, as even I had stopped going in. Doing any work was pointless because there was no one to submit it to, no one pushing the content through to be laid out for print or the website. We had not put a paper on the stands in almost three weeks.

I could have gone out and looked for another job at that point, but it seemed useless and like I would only have the same experience anywhere else. People had stopped showing up for work everywhere, and the effects of The Shot could already be seen rolling through many parts of the culture.

If only things had stopped there.

The Shot—which can refer both to the substance itself and the syringes in which it is placed—is a velvety green goop with a thick consistency somewhere between that of toothpaste and maple syrup. Its appearance is not so different from the stuff they used to make called "tire slime," a runny glue-like liquid with a lumpy texture sold in a plastic tube that could be squeezed into a bike tire to prevent punctures and fill small holes.

Users will fill a special syringe with The Shot—the needles feature an extra wide opening to accommodate the passage of the thick gunk—and shoot it not into their arms, but into their *stomachs*. Somewhere along the line, by way of extensive personal experimentation by the users, the stomach has been discovered to be the most effective place to inject The Shot. It produces the most vibrant high, apparently, more so than the arm or thigh or heel. Whether this has anything to do with the digestive system, I don't know.

It's disgusting to watch them shoot up, ramming the needle into their soft pink bellies as if they were diabetics only minutes away from death, pumping their bodies full of life-saving insulin. Most don't even flinch when the needle goes in. The prick of pain is but a small price to pay for the bounty about to swirl through their veins. Once The Shot is pulsing through their system, users' eyes glaze over and they no longer seem to see what is in front of them. Their pupils grow wide and fade to a deeper shade of black like camera lenses, empty and dead. It is as if they are seeing everything and nothing at once; still themselves, and yet completely gone.

Apart from the vacant look in their eyes and the curious, spirit-fueled rants that begin flowing from their mouths, a user high on The Shot is *almost* indistinguishable from a regular person. And yet, their personalities seem to disappear, floating away for a while to a place behind the scenes of consciousness to be replaced by something unsettling and artificial. Beneath that, something sinister. As for the physical effects, The Shot produces no slurring of speech, no hindrance to motor function, no uncontrollable giggling, sudden depression, or incoherence. In fact, a user's awareness seems *heightened* in a way, as if they suddenly see deeper and farther and clearer into the universe than the rest of us. One of the perks, they say, is that "everything you see becomes something else." That's *always* what they say; *all* of them, that exact same phrase—word for word and without fail.

Everything you see becomes something else.

I have not experienced the effects of The Shot myself, but I think I've got the gist of it. Users describe the sensation as a hallucination *of sorts*. It does not sound like a "trip" similar to that of LSD or hallucinogenic mushrooms, where Warron Zevon might visit you for a conversation about *An American*

Werewolf in London or Raphael reaches down from a Ninja Turtles poster on the wall and offers to light your cigarette. Users of The Shot are aware of their surroundings and can identify the objects around them—though incorrectly, at times.

For example: cups. Any sort of cup—whether a pint glass, a child's sipping cup, a coffee mug, or a disposable paper cone from a water dispenser—is described by users of The Shot as a chalice. *The* chalice, in fact, "of our Lord Jesus Christ, born of The Blessed Mother." If it is something you can drink out of, in a user's eyes, it's the cup of Christ. The Holy Grail. I've seen users take this part to such an extreme that they will refuse to drink from a cup while high out of reverence, opting instead for a water bottle or slurping out of a bowl, deeming themselves unworthy to even touch their lips to an object so sacred. If fifteen or twenty different cups are all lined up in a row, each of the cups is still *the* chalice; each one still holy. The concept that this could not logically be possible evades their compromised minds.

These side-effects were intriguing in the early days, even humorous at times. That was back when people were using The Shot only once a day or so, the highs lasting for four to six hours. But things have progressed substantially since then.

Dear God, how they've progressed.

I do not understand how something can exist so prominently—so *loudly*—on the earth and be in daily use by so many human beings—*millions* of human beings—and yet we know almost *nothing* about it. And the fact that no one seems to be even slightly *concerned* about that anymore? It is nothing short of madness. And just how the hell is there so *much* of it?

That's another thing: the flow and availability of The

Shot never wavers. Wherever its source lies, the supply refuses to dry up.

*

Back in Year One, The Shot rocketed to the forefront of the public's attention when a prominent actor named Glenn Champlain (an A-lister and multiple-time Academy Award nominee) recorded a webcam video of himself while high, then uploaded it to YouTube.

The video consisted of Champlain ranting—or preaching, more like—at his laptop camera for more than an hour and a half. At a total run-time of 118 minutes, he had created a home movie that rivaled the length of his feature films. In the middle of his wild recording was a 28-minute section where he became completely silent, staring blankly into the lens. Somewhere between 01:12:00 and 01:13:00, it's as if he reawakens, or comes back to the present from some other place. He shakes his head, blinks several times, then resumes his speech at full speed.

He uploaded the video, tweeted it out to his plethora of followers, and within two hours YouTube crashed because of all the people trying to watch it at once. News networks cut together compilations of the most eyebrow-raising sections and replayed the clips endlessly. Social media lit up with their own mass-commentary, suggesting the actor's possible loss of sanity, speculating on what this "shot" was to which he kept referring, seeming to relish in watching his career take a very public dive before their eyes. Numerous comparisons were made to Charlie Sheen's meltdown in 2011. People did not seem to be concerned or freaked out by Champlain's bizarre behavior (as I was); they treated it like a joke, much the same as they did The Shot itself only a few months later.

For several weeks, Glenn was the laughingstock of the country, and much of the world. Those with more sympathy pointed out that he did not seem the sort to humiliate himself like this, and that he was usually a very private person, not a figure obsessed with constantly placing himself in the spotlight. Prior to his meltdown video, he had been considered by his celebrity peers to be a reserved, cordial, hospitable man of utmost professionalism. That sort of thing was rare in show business.

The following is an excerpt from the video transcription, compiled and published by Titan Media Group.

"People, how have we even existed this long without The Shot? What we've been doing… people, my friends, brothers and sisters, that's not living. The Shot is living. It's beyond living, it's beyond seeing, a gift to mankind, and we are the generation blessed enough to have it gifted to us from on high! I mean, do you understand *how incredible this is, people? We are the flock and have indeed been tended to by some gracious shepherd, fed and nurtured and now given a great reward.*

"The Shot is the richest gift ever awarded to mankind, sweeter than honey, more pure than gold. A gift from The Mother Herself. God, a higher power, a supreme being, whatever you want to call it. Mother Nature, creation or the cosmos or fate or whatever name you want to give it. Maybe it bubbled up out of the earth or poured forth from a rock like when our Father Moses got upset at the people of Israel and smote the stone with his staff, causing water to run freely. Or maybe, maybe a femur bone was thrown into the air by an ancient race of ape-men, suspended and spinning until it evolved into a space vessel, The Mothership, *then our sweet Mother concocted this elemental bliss for us from aboard Her starship! And The Shot*

has just been stewing and brewing for thousands or hundreds of thousands or millions of years until She had the recipe just right, until it was perfected and ready. Ready for us."

Without transition or any break in his speech, he would change subjects. This happened numerous times throughout the video.

"Those lights, man… I mean, just look at those lights! The stars out your window, have you seen them? I mean, they're right there, have you really taken a look and seen them? Just like Our Mother said in Her holy word, 'And the heavens were opened, and behold…'

"Oh yes, just look at them…"

A long pause. At this point he gazed off-screen for a while.

"It's like… it's like going on a magic carpet ride and being presented with the best ideas that have ever crossed your mind! It expands the channels of the brain, people, do you know what I'm saying? It unfolds the deeper layers of our grey matter that have been crammed closed and dormant for so long. I mean, this has got to be the best thing to ever happen to our collective consciousness! It is A GIFT to the world. No, no, that's not big enough. The whole universe will be blessed by what The Shot can give us, much like the blessing that spilled over to every nation from the offspring of Abraham's loins. What a great fortune has befallen us! We, a wicked and slanderous generation, have been shown grace upon grace, deep to deep, as if a teardrop has been plucked from the very eyes of YHWH in heaven and planted at our feet."

At this point, he moved his face even closer to the web camera and held unblinking eye contact with the lens, as if pleading with each and every viewer personally.

"Will you, too, partake of this most blessed cup? To reject it—oh friends—to reject it is to reject great wellsprings of riches

of the mind and soul and body and heart. To cast it away is to deny new landscapes of understanding, new frontiers of wisdom. To turn your back on The Shot is 'to have eyes and not see, to have ears and not hear.'

"And do you not....

Another long pause. He made a strained face, as if in extreme pain, gritting his teeth and balling his hands into tight fists next to his temples. When he released this pose, there were tears on his cheeks and he resumed eye contact with a look of deep concern.

"Friends, do you not want *to be prepared for The Ship? Our blessed mother hen comes for us. She will scoop us up to safety in Her warm and loving wings and carry us off of this scarred and broken terra to deliver us to the kingdom of lights! And only by The Shot will you truly see this. Only through The Shot will you truly hear this. The Mothership's arrival is imminent."*

And so on. It is worth noting that Champlain had previously never been known to speak of faith or religion whatsoever, other than stating once in an interview that he considered himself an atheist. And yet, while on The Shot he was suddenly quite versed in biblical concepts and was quoting Scripture, or at least some convoluted version of it.

It eventually became the most-shared, most-watched video ever, clocking in at just over four and a half billion views within two months of being uploaded (beating out the formerly most-watched video—a ridiculous but admittedly catchy pop hit by a South Korean rapper—by almost double). A representative from YouTube confirmed that the play count was authentic—not fabricated by bots, as has been known to happen—and that their analytics showed that the link had been visited by more than three billion unique IP addresses, meaning that, not accounting for those who had watched the video more than once, roughly one half of the world's population had witnessed the actor's drug-addled rant.

Renowned anthropologists conducted extensive studies on the video's cultural impact. A bestselling book deconstructing the video and Champlain's behavior was penned by a highly-respected professor of psychology from Stanford University. The religious community chimed in as prominent ministers of Lutheran, Methodist, and Baptist churches, as well several rabbis and Catholic priests all gave their hearty disapproval of the actor's many spiritually-charged statements, citing them as theologically errant and even heretical. One pastor of a mega-church in Houston, Texas, went so far as to write a pamphlet for his congregation titled "THE DEVIL IS ALIVE AND WELL ON YOUTUBE: 77 Fallacies with 'The Champlain Video,' and the *Real* Meaning of the Scriptures Misquoted Therein." This pamphlet was made available as a free PDF on the church's website, and gained some significant traction within the Christian blogosphere.

Online community boards for fans of the video emerged, and meet-up groups were formed. People would get together and watch the video in its entirety in a communal setting, usually while getting high (although not on The Shot, at least not at first), then analyze it together afterwards.

I heard about even stranger things, such as groups that would organize public showings of the video at local art house cinemas, but they would only watch the twenty-eight minute silent section. They would crank up the volume so that the white noise was blaring, and they would try to blink as infrequently as possible for the duration of the presentation, soaking up every possible clue or meaning, getting lost in Glenn's blank eyes as if he was communicating something secret to them without words.

It goes without saying that the "Illuminati" subculture on YouTube had a heyday breaking down and analyzing the video frame by frame. As far as bizarre events went, it was their Holy Grail.

The whole thing became more than just a famous person's public meltdown, more than just a laughable news story about another drug-addled member of ultra-privileged society losing their shit. Those who did not criticize Champlain treated his words like those of a prophet, something transcendent and ominous, too important to be ignored. There were people who had entire sections of the monologue memorized and I would hear it recited between friends in coffee shops, at barstools, on the bus. Quotations from the video started showing up around the city, spray-painted boldly on the sides of buildings or train cars. "THE SHOT IS LIVING. IT'S BEYOND LIVING. A GIFT TO MANKIND," or "WILL YOU TOO PARTAKE OF THIS MOST BLESSED CUP?" and even "THE MOTHERSHIP'S ARRIVAL IS IMMINENT". Seeing these quotes blazoned across walls in public areas—always in bright, neon green paint with letters that bled—was unnerving. I believe that people meant them to be celebratory, like proclamations of some wonderful paradigm shift in our culture, but to me they seemed foreboding and out of place. It reminded me of graffiti in a graphic novel I read once; violent black letters slashed onto storefronts that said things like, "THE END IS NIGH," and, "WHO WATCHES THE WATCHMEN?" I felt like, maybe, the Doomsday Clock was ticking a little bit closer to midnight.

Regardless of peoples' opinions for or against Glenn Champlain, the question on everyone's lips was: "Just *what* is this 'Shot' he keeps referring to?" He used the term more than 160 times in the course of the video, always with the functioning word "The" in front of it. It wasn't just *a* shot, but "*The* Shot."

Nearly every news network in the country reported as having tried to reach Champlain for comment and explanation once the clips were in heavy rotation on TV and online. The trouble was that he was found dead by his agent two days after posting the video, in the very same room that he had recorded the rant. The coroner's report estimated that he had taken his own life shortly after putting the video online, as the time of death correlated approximately with the time that the video went live.

It was a suicide by hanging, and he left a four-word letter:

Gone to The Mothership

In the days since, The Shot has very rarely been associated with suicide. From what I have gleaned, most users do not hold to the belief that taking one's own life will deliver them automatically to The Mothership—the vessel they believe to be waiting in some nearby galaxy that will eventually arrive to welcome them aboard and carry them home to "paradise." Champlain's fatal decision is considered among most users to have been a poor one. He simply allowed himself to become too excited and impatient for his reward, they say. He was immature in his belief and got carried away. It is widely accepted in the ideology of The Shot that users must wait patiently for The Mothership. This is something I learned from talking to enough of them in the early days when they were still safe to be around. They say that the ship will arrive when the timing is right—when *She* deems it right, in Her infinite wisdom—and that regular use of The Shot will further educate users on the principles of interstellar travel, thus preparing them to board the ship.

There *is* no ship, of course.

There cannot be, logically. The concept is impossible and absurd. The idea that there is some sort of motherly spacecraft coming to redeem mankind is nothing more than another wacky religious sham conjured—probably in some laboratory—to stir up the hearts and betray the hopes of degenerates seeking comfort in life, an answer to "What It All Means." The Mothership is an imaginary savior, nothing more than a new blend of religious fanaticism in a long line of weird belief systems.

Oh yes, and those news networks that wanted to ask Champlain what The Shot was all about? They did not have to wait long for an answer. Only weeks after the video was posted, preloaded syringes of The Shot could be found for sale in nearly every back alley (heck, every street corner, for that matter) from Los Angeles to Long Beach, if you knew the right person to ask. The substance had caused a man to kill himself and talk about some seriously crazy shit, so naturally, instead of staying the hell away from it at all costs, the more "experimental" public wanted to see for themselves just what The Shot was capable of.

SIX

The first time that I actually witnessed someone use The Shot in person scared the hell out of me (though, in retrospect, it was mild in comparison to what I have seen since).

This was somewhere around the end of Year One, perhaps early Year Two, after The Shot had gained some notoriety but was not yet in mass public consumption. The user was Jake, a good friend at the time, and while he and I would occasionally smoke weed or eat shrooms while watching eighties horror films together (*Halloween III: Season of the Witch* was a personal favorite, as well as *Pumpkinhead* and *Re-animator*), neither of us were frequent drug users. That said, when The Shot was being used and raved about by our circle of friends and we were seeing it exchange hands in our own neighborhood, Jake's interest was piqued. I think that he probably recognized on some level that using it was unwise, what with all the unknowns about the substance, but he was too captivated by the wild stories our friends would tell.

Jake acquired a few ounces of The Shot through some source or another—it was inexpensive and easy to come by, even then—and called me excitedly to come over for what would be his first experience with the drug.

I went over to Jake's place that evening—a second-floor apartment in a third-rate complex—and we settled in on his comfortable thrift store couch, surrounded by secondhand lamps that would have been better suited in the home of somebody's grandmother in the 1970's. There were posters on the wall for *Scarface*, Bob Marley and the

Wailers, a young, Mohawk-clad Robert De Niro, and a faded flag that featured the artwork from *Dark Side of the Moon.*

From out of a repurposed jar that once held Gerber baby food (one of many ways the sellers packaged and distributed The Shot at the time. Not all of them were so courteous as to pre-load the needles), Jake loaded the green gunk into the back of the syringe by scooping a gob of it onto his finger and shoving one glistening bead at a time into the plastic tube. He did this messily at first, but with increasing skill.

"I've watched a few people do this before," Jake said, "although they were a hell of a lot better at it. I'm making a mess, this shit is *sticky.*"

Then, with shaking hands, he held the full syringe up to the light and flicked at it thrice to get rid of any air pockets. The incandescent light from his lamp caused the slime within to illuminate with an ominous green glow.

He held out the readied instrument, offering it to me. "Let's trip out at the same time, man! We'll both take some. Do it together."

I looked at the syringe, slightly mesmerized by the attractive bright green color of the substance inside; enchanted with the way it glistened in its tube and gave off a glossy shine when it caught the light. The needle itself looked sharp and clean, gleaming like a tiny sword. My right hand twitched and almost reached out to take the syringe from him. Some part of me thought better of this.

"You... you go ahead, man," I said. "I'll just watch this time, in case anything weird happens. Wouldn't want us both to have a bad trip or something."

And, Jesus... *that* was the best decision I've ever made.

Something weird *did* happen: Jake disappeared. At least, Jake *as I knew him* disappeared.

He lifted his shirt to expose the soft white skin of his belly, a thin crosshatching of curved black hair quivered below his bellybutton. He took a deep breath and pierced the needle into himself, wincing as the metal poked through his flesh.

I remember having an intense gagging sensation when I watched Jake push down on the syringe's plunger, forcing the green slime out of its tube and into his body; everything about it looked unnatural and wrong. I swallowed hard and willed the contents of my stomach to remain where they were.

He pulled the needle out and winced again, sucking in a quick breath through clenched teeth. He used a Burger King napkin to dab at the small bead of blood that had bubbled on his skin. He looked at me, a question in his expression. We just stared at each other for a moment.

"Nothing's happening yet," Jake said. "Did I do it right?"

"Don't ask me, man," I said.

His eyes widened suddenly. I could *see* the expansion of his pupils as they grew wider and deeper black. It reminded me of the way the Great White's eyes looked in *Jaws*, right before he bit a boat in half and dragged a bloodied Quint into the sea.

"*Whoooa*," Jake said, looking out the window.

"What is it?" I asked, leaning in, scooting closer to him on the couch. "What do you see?"

"Man… those *stars*, look at them!" Jake said.

The only view from his window was the other crummy apartment building across the courtyard, lit in ugly orange light by sodium vapor lamps. No part of the night sky was visible from the angle at which we sat. Even if it had been, the stars would have been obscured by clouds and city lights.

"There aren't any stars, Jake. Not that we can see from here, man," I said.

He ignored me and said, "You know, I hope that window is properly sealed for interstellar travel. If it cracked and broke, the force of the suction and the freezing, oxygen-less vacuum of space would kill us within seconds. We'd suffocate, or turn into human-shaped ice blocks. Both, probably." Jake squinted his eyes thoughtfully, and nodded his head in agreement with his own words.

He went on. "But I don't think that will happen. That window *must* be sealed. And that glass *has* to be thick and tempered, like on a space station. Aluminum silicate and fused silica glass. Strong stuff. Yes, She would know what we need to be kept safe. She knows even when a single sparrow falls, so how much more is She faithful to provide for us?"

"*She*, Jake? Who are you talking about?" I asked.

"The Mothership," he said.

My stomach fluttered with sickness and dread, but at the time I was not sure why.

"Like Champlain talked about," I said flatly, as much to myself as to Jake. "But why a *ship*, Jake? You're talking about a 'she,' like it's a person."

Jake raised his hands and made a frame in the air with his thumbs and forefingers, the way a director might demonstrate the viewpoint from which he wanted a scene to be filmed. He took on an elderly, reverent tone and said, "…and the woman was adorned in purple and scarlet gowns, arrayed with finest gold and jewels and pearls, holding in her hand a golden chalice filled with all blessings and knowledge and *pleasure!* And she rode atop a silver chariot, a great shining *beast*, upon which was writ everyone's names, the names of those foreordained to be redeemed and carried away by the sleek and mighty behemoth! Her vessel of *glory!*"

"Jake is that... was that something *from the Bible?*" I asked. Jake had never so much as fluttered the pages of a Bible or darkened the doorway of a church, as far as I knew, and he was the furthest thing from religious.

I Googled some of what he said later, from memory. It was from Revelation chapter 17, though Jake grossly misquoted and changed it. The beast in the real passage is scarlet, not silver. And it does not bring blessings or glory. Quite the opposite.

"It was given to me from the tongue of our Most Blessed Mother," Jake answered, and stretched his hand out towards the window. "How I long to be with Her... But the sweetness of the vision which She has just imparted to me— oh, *the joy!*—is enough to give me patience, to tide me over until that wonderful day of fruition comes. She will come, yes. She will come in Her own perfect timing, and gather Her chicks into the glorious fold. And to think, *I am one of Her own!* Oh, it's beautiful, Matthias, *so beautiful.*"

My name is not Matthias.

"All right Jake, I think you're just having a weird trip," I said, although that's not what I was really thinking. "I'll get you some water. Just hang tight. Ride it out until you come down a little."

I stood up from the couch and made for the kitchen, but Jake leapt in front of me and clamped his hands onto my arms in a tight grip. His eyes were wide, watery, and vacant as he stared wildly into mine.

"Matthias! You must taste, *you must see!* It is too lovely, too wonderful to overlook. This great gift—*OH!*—what a gift we've been given! Here here here, we will ready The Shot for you, you must take some too."

Again with that talk of gifts, I thought. *Just like Glenn Champlain.*

Jake snatched the empty syringe from the coffee table and cradled it in one hand like a delicate treasure. "Please, Matthias. Open your eyes with me. Then you too will see! Do you not want to see?"

"Jake, calm down. No, I *do not* want to 'see,' okay? I just want you to ride out your high, and then we're flushing the rest of that Shot shit down the toilet."

"NO!" Jake screamed, and shook me violently. "You fool! How dare you suggest such a travesty, such utter madness! Tell me, Matthias, would you flush *gold?* Would you throw finest diamonds of knowledge and wisdom into *the garbage?* Would you hold the key of life in your very palm and cast it *into the sea?* Matthias, The Shot *is* that key, our path unto higher truth and understanding! We need it we need it we need it we need it *we need it.*" He was breathing fast and hard where he stood, nearly hyperventilating. His chest heaved, his shoulders raised and lowered rapidly with each breath. "Please, please, take some too, just *try* some, fill your veins with this sweet nectar and then you will *see!* Oh, Matthias, I want you to see!"

"Let *go* of me, Jake," I said, firmly. "I am not taking any, so stop asking. And stop calling me Matthias, you know my name. You're just shit-faced, all right? Sit down and chill. You need to ride this thing out."

All at once, Jake's arms relaxed and his face melted into a look of complete serenity. He sat back down, and turned his gaze again towards the window. He stared out of it as if no altercation between us had just occurred.

Jake did not speak again for several hours.

I brought him water and tried to get him to drink it (not that it would do a single thing to counteract the effects of The Shot, I realize now), but he pushed it away when I held it to his lips. I snapped my fingers in front of his face, said his name over and over, even slapped him lightly on the cheeks. No response. He only stared out the window, wide-eyed and unblinking, the small pouches of skin beneath his eyes twitching occasionally. For lack of a better term, Jake looked *starry eyed*, as if he was seeing the most beautiful, marvelous display of his life, and only death by starvation would peel him away from that perfect sight. Maybe not even that.

I stayed with him, and eventually I fell asleep on the arm of the couch.

When he came to four hours later, I stirred awake. Jake was looking around the room, blinking and rubbing his eyes. He looked confused, like his own apartment was a place he knew he ought to recognize, but had not been there in a very long time. He turned to me and smiled.

"So, was it weird? What did I do? Did I freak out? Man, I don't remember anything."

I stared at him, still drowsy.

"Except..." he continued, "maybe something about a ship?"

*

The Shot is, somehow, endlessly available. And yet, nobody ever knows where it comes from, how it is made (if it is even "made" at all), or who gets it from whom.

There was a period of time—end of Year Three, early Year Four? Somewhere around there—when I made an exhaustive effort to follow the chain of distributors as far backwards down the line as I possibly could, asking one dealer or another (sometimes forcefully—these were hardly "tough guys") from whom they got their supply. I would then approach *that* higher-up dealer, then the next higher-up, and so on. Often, my questions just led me in circles, looping back around to the same people. Even more often, they led to completely dead ends, or fake names.

These distributors were not drug dealers in the traditional, old-world sense (old-world meaning: before The Shot); sleazy low-lifes in gaudy pimp glasses and baggy coats who would hang around high schools, shopping malls, and back alleys, thinking they were concealing their occupation. Dealers of The Shot were more like friendly clerks at the neighborhood convenience store (except that they sold one product and one product only). These were just regular joes next door who would wave to you in the street or knock on your door, who knew your name, who would ask how you were doing—and mean it—then say they were just checking in to see if you were all stocked up, if you needed anything. There was not even competition between them, nor any reason for it. It was like they were all on the same team, or all had the same boss. Users knew if they needed more of The Shot, a reasonably-priced seller with a genuine smile would not be hard to find. Since The Shot was never made illegal, the distributors were able to operate in the open.

The Shot used to be sold in reusable containers (like Jake's baby food jar), usually in portions of three to ten ounces, an amount that at one time would have lasted a casual user a few days to a week. You would see people pulling out these containers in public; herbal tinctures filled with The Shot, or orange plastic prescription bottles, mason jars, Ziploc bags, small tin tubs that once held hand salve, even plastic soap dispensers with a layer of filmy gunk on them. Any sort of compact and sealable container would do. Some of the "classier" users had hand-crafted cases of pristine leather or fine silver that held syringes pre-loaded with The Shot; five green, glossy tubes of madness all in a neat row.

But these days, the walk-around dealers selling The Shot in recycled containers are long since obsolete. When people started realizing that there were no laws governing the use or sale of The Shot (oh, sure, laws were proposed in Years One and Two, but none ever materialized), and that there were not going to be any laws governing it anytime soon, then the brick-and-mortar stores started popping up.

Now there are Shot-exclusive dispensaries—scores, hundreds, probably thousands of them across the country. There's that saying about having "one on every street corner," but... seriously. It can be purchased in many different container sizes (factory-sealed and food-grade sanitary) for a relatively consistent price-per-ounce. If one shop tried to gouge the price (which only happened for about two weeks before the store owners realized it was pointless), any user would know well enough that they could purchase their fix for a reasonable price somewhere else within walking distance, so why bother marking it up?

The fact that The Shot is now sold in stores—and the fact that almost all stores are now exclusively retailers of The Shot and nothing else—is one of the most confounding, infuriating, *fucking ridiculous* things about this whole arrangement. Where the hell are they getting all of it? Where does it all come from? Do they just order it up from some mass distributor? Do they even have to buy their inventory, or does the product just keep showing up, palletized in truckloads from some mysterious source? Is there a company that has somehow managed to fly under the radar while producing and distributing billions of pounds of it without ever coming into the spotlight? Or maybe the maker of the product is under airtight government protection and concealed from the public eye. It's not as if there are different "brands" of The Shot. It's all the same stuff no matter where you get it from. Some stores will put their own labels on the product—homemade stickers specific to the region or local culture that are always decorated with excited fonts and jovial illustrations in various shades of green—but the copy and content of the labels are almost always exactly the same. No nutrition facts, no daily values, no manufacturer information, and exactly one listed ingredient.

I'll let you guess what that is.

There is no age restriction for use—so, yes, *kids* are taking it now, *little* kids, shooting it into their stomachs on the couch right alongside mom and dad, then the whole family trips out together and has disturbing discussions about the cornucopia of joys en route to them from The Mothership.

There are no nutrition facts, nor is there a suggested serving size. Oddly enough, it seems to be quite impossible to overdose on The Shot. Oh yes, our wonderful culture built on excess and gluttony has certainly *tried* to take too much of it, but The Shot's absorption into the body seems to have a very definite stopping point. Inject one syringe or plunge an entire 16 oz. jar into your system and the effect will be precisely the same: a four to six hour high with an almost immediate drop-off. Users come off of The Shot instantly once the hallucinatory buzz has run its course, and like Jake, they usually don't remember anything about the experience. Thus, most users load up for another round immediately, cycling through either four or six injections in a twenty-four hour period so that they remain in a constant state of Shot-induced thinking.

I have done some personal experimenting on The Shot, using poor-man's methods that could hardly be called scientific, but the results were telling just the same. The Shot will not boil or burn, nor will it freeze. No matter the elements to which it is exposed, it remains at a steady temperature of 68 to 72 degrees Fahrenheit. Also, it cannot effectively be diluted down, added to, or mixed with any other substance.

Around the time that Jake had his first trip, I watched users at parties rolling marijuana around in The Shot, coating the buds in the green slime, then trying to smoke the whole sticky mess. That did nothing but ruin the weed and leave a puddle of untouched Shot in the bowl of the glass pipe. Others tried to pair The Shot with cocaine, methamphetamine, LSD, crushed pills, alcohol, and all manner of other things (including trying to bake it into edibles), and no amount of stirring or blending or pounding will allow the other substance to merge with The Shot. The green gook pulsates and shimmies ever so slightly, as if it's a living thing (remember the purple slime in *Ghostbusters II*?), until it has forced out the foreign matter, "purifying" itself, so to speak. This is a truly bizarre process to witness. For lack of a better term, The Shot appears to literally *excrete* whatever was trying to mix with it. The substance is an anomaly in every sense of the word.

FIVE

During Year Three, when the U.S. and U.K. were blissfully hooked and The Shot was catching fire in the Eastern half of the world, I formed a sort of anti-Shot group that met in secrecy. It was a small community (a *very* small community, because we were already the minority population by this point) of Shot-abstinent people that met regularly to discuss what was happening in the world, where life and culture might be headed, what that might eventually mean for non-users, and what, if anything, the few of us could do about it.

There were about fifteen of us to begin with, mostly people I had found on Craigslist or other online forums by publishing very carefully-worded posts. These posts had to be phrased in such a way so as to not raise a red flag to a user—*A GROUP OPPOSED TO THE SHOT! HOW DARE!*—but still leave apparent breadcrumbs for a non-user to pick up on. I would post headings like "Open Conversations of The Shot, The Mothership, and Beyond." That one still comes across as if it is tailored to users, but my hope was that non-users would be most interested in the "Beyond." Another was "Questions About Glory, Salvation, and The Blessed Mother: Is The Shot Really The Answer?" A user would take one look at a heading like that and think something along the lines of "Well, *of course* it is. Good for those brothers and sisters leading unconvinced sheep into the fold," when really I was hoping that non-users would pick up on the doubtful question. And they did.

We few met weekly in each others' apartments for a number of months, hop-scotching the location from one to another each time. Not a lot of brainstorming or scheming ended up happening about how to halt the growth and spread of The Shot, even though that had been my original intention. We mostly just talked, bonding together over how insane the world had become. I think everyone was relieved (I certainly was) just to have a space to talk to "regular" humans for a little while, and not have to pretend we knew Scripture and put on our praise-the-Mothership faces like we did in public everyday.

It was mostly people my age, twenty- or thirty-somethings, but a few older than that. Other than not using The Shot, we all had another thing in common: having to leave our previous jobs, and in some cases take on Shot-related occupations. There was a former barista, Jonah, who worked as a cashier at a Shot shop. Morgan had been in her final year of law school—top of her class and all queued up for an internship at a major firm—when all of the sudden people stopped suing each other or committing crimes; people on The Shot were far too satisfied to worry about petty things like suing their spouses or robbing convenience stores. She, too, worked at a Shot shop (it was about the only job that existed anymore). Glenn, one of our older members, had been a civil engineer with the DOT for over thirty-seven years (and only two more away from a hearty pension awaiting him) when he and two thousand of his fellow civil servants were told to go home one day without explanation. Glenn had said most of his buddies had taken up The Shot in the wake of their lay-off—better than drinking themselves to death, he supposed—but that the green stuff had always "given him the willies." There was also Melody, David, Casey, Janine. The others' names have faded from my memory...

That was a pleasant time for me, as pleasant as it could have been under the circumstances. The group gave me hope that something could still be done to turn things back around for humanity. If there were a few level-headed people to be found in my own community, surely there would be others across the rest of the country, and the world. We all agreed (for a time) that use of The Shot was madness. We had watched it consume our families (two older brothers, a younger sister, and both parents in my case, plus all the extended relatives), devolve our society (with the closing down of power, water, gas, and sewage utilities, among other things), and simplify the minds of our race into a stupid solitary pursuit: take The Shot, and keep taking it.

I had a crush on Janine for a little while. She had pale, lightly-freckled skin with natural blushes of pink on both cheeks, as if she were perpetually coming in from the cold. She was one of those girls with straight, nothing-special brown hair, and yet it made her features more pretty than plain. She had worked at a secondhand bookstore called A Novel Idea, but users only read one book, the Bible, and there were not enough non-using customers to keep the place open. The owner (a user herself) told Janine one day not to come back into work anymore. The woman locked up A Novel Idea and never returned, leaving thousands of volumes untouched on the shelves inside. Janine told me how, several days later, she had gotten a wheelbarrow and used her own key to go in through the back door. She piled the wheelbarrow high with heaps of books and made a number of trips back and forth from the shop to her own apartment, stockpiling as many of the abandoned copies as she could fit in her place. When she found out that I liked to read, she would bring me paperbacks at every meeting; Ray Bradbury, Isaac Asimov, Philip K. Dick. She liked "the weird, science-y stuff," so she called it.

I pretended to like those books as an excuse to talk more with Janine, but actually they filled me with dread. It was not that they weren't any good as far as stories go, but rather that they presented visions of worlds that were dangerous, abnormal, unsafe. Some of the books had Kafkaesque government systems that oppressed their people for bizarre and illogical reasons, dystopian societies built on fear and strange rules and delicate boundaries. Then there were the characters who were just plain mad... Science fiction ought to be escapism, and those books reminded me too much of life in the present.

Ultimately, not even our quaint little group of holdouts was immune to The Shot's inexplicable allure.

We had been meeting together about nine months when the numbers began to dwindle. People would stop showing up, would not return my calls or emails. A few of them disappeared from their homes or apartments without a word—I checked. We were friends one day and strangers the next. The scariest part was not knowing if they had simply started using The Shot of their own volition and abandoned the rest of us (which was bad), or if they had been found out by the users and forced into taking The Shot (which was *really* bad).

In less than a year's time, the group had completely dissolved. I lost contact with everyone, including Janine. It stung terribly, having enjoyed a brief time of fellowship, of real life, of hope for the future, then being reduced back down to just me in my apartment, alone. Maybe, my mind suggested, everyone just moved away, or had a family emergency in another city... *yeah, right*. Maybe they decided it was simply too dangerous to keep meeting or to go outside, so they were all holed up indoors like me. If that was the case, I could not really blame them for it.

It was Janine's disappearance that troubled me the most, not only because I felt that we had a sincere connection that I had hoped would lead to something long term, but also because it was so out of character for her to vanish without a word, without explanation. I liked her, and she had liked me too, I'm certain of it. And she stuck with the group longer than anyone, even when it was down to just the two of us. Then it wasn't a group so much as a chance for us to hang out together and talk about books and our former lives and offer a few token comments about how to rid the world of The Shot even though that wasn't what we were interested in talking about anymore.

But then one day, she didn't come.

I called and texted her a dozen times before going over to her apartment. The door was left open a crack, and inside were all the books she had taken from A Novel Idea, piled high against the walls in uneven stacks. There's no way she would have taken off without bringing at least some of these, I thought. All of her other belongings were there too. She had left her clothes, her food, her furniture. I closed and locked the door and slept on her couch that night, and for the next three nights. She did not return, so I went home and tried not to dwell upon the inevitable truth.

The users had gotten to her, and there was nothing I could do about it. I would have gone after her, but she could have been anywhere by that point. Even if I had, she would not have been herself anymore. She was already one of them.

I do not go outside much anymore, and when I do it's only to scrounge for food, water, or supplies.

The city's water purification plant and sewage facilities

went from being unreliable to being completely non-functional. They shut down around the same time Glenn from our group lost his job with the DOT, and that was Year *Two*, so at this point I've had no clean water from the tap and no ability to flush a toilet in three years. Water is simply not a priority for users anymore (The Shot makes it such that their bodies no longer need it). I am reduced to finding bottled water to drink and cook with, which is not impossible, but it is only sporadically available. Some of the abandoned grocery stores will still have a few dusty cases left in their back storage rooms, but in three years' time I've pretty well cleared out every supermarket supply room in a five mile radius.

Food is a little easier to find, for now. One can live off of non-perishables for quite a while. That is, until those non-perishables cross their expiration dates and make the transformation into *perishables*. Even canned soup and vegetables only last about four or five years before they become stagnant and sour in their metal containers. I have not seen or tasted a fresh vegetable, a piece of non-canned fruit, a loaf of bread, or a cut of real meat in more than two years.

There are actually a few places left that still sell "food," but their menus consist of nothing but the two following items: artificially flavored cheesy chips (made of something other than potatoes or corn, because *those* resources are gone), and chocolate chip cookies pumped full of fake ingredients. The only thing I can chalk this up to is a weird form of "the munchies" that occurs in some users, though not all of them. Maybe chips and cookies are like a reminiscent thing for them; those salty and refined sugar treats with zero nutritional value that remind users of that unenlightened, long ago time when they actually had to put food in their mouths for sustenance. Most of them do not eat or drink anything, *ever*. They don't have to anymore, The Shot sustains them, like some perfect superfood.

Infuriatingly, a lot of the users even look in better physical shape than ever before; more muscular, thinner, toned, their features more defined (despite the fact that there is no longer a single exercise club or workout gym to be found open for business), all as a benefit of dieting on nothing but The Shot. I mean, it might sound shallow to point this out as if it were actually a *benefit* of using, but I'm saying that it is not rational how *good* people look. Their bodies are in shape in a purely Hollywood sense, which is to say not necessarily healthy or authentic, but holding up the appearance of sexiness even if what lies beneath is a deception, like silicone propping up loose skin. Skin looks clearer, teeth look whiter, jawlines and breasts alike have become firmer. Those once unattractive and homely are now gorgeous and ruddy. Humans as a whole have become a glorified, perfected, Garden of Eden sort of version of themselves.

Far behind us are the days of Whole Foods-propelled propaganda of organic *everything*, of eating only raw foods and quinoa and kale and some new magic berries that Dr. Oz discovered to zap fat people into skinny people in only three weeks. Users just *do not* eat anymore. Why didn't we think of *that* diet forever ago? Speaking of fat, you don't see a lot of obese people these days, which in another time and place would have been considered a good change of pace for our country.

But here's the thing about being surrounded by a physically flawless population: we have all of these gorgeous people running around, yet nobody is having sex anymore. The Shot has consumed all interest in copulating, whether for procreating or pleasure, as far as I can tell. Not that I have undergone an extensive investigation of this in particular, but the clues are pretty out in the open. For example, there aren't any babies around, or little kids for that matter. The youngest people I have seen in a long time were at least ten or eleven years old (which, if you do the math, means they probably started taking The Shot with Mom and Dad around age *four or five*). Apart from the lack of babies, men and women do not put off an air of having the slightest interest in being together romantically, nor in hooking up, seeking relationships, or even in having a good fuck. Talk of that ever-pending Mothership from the skies is to them a wholly more exhilarating exchange.

*

My friend Jake was animated about trying to convince me to take The Shot with him on his first go-round, but after his continued use and abuse of the substance over the following months, his passion turned to argument, then ultimately to demand.

The final time I was at Jake's place, he said (not for the first time), "Matthias, you really *need* to take The Shot with me. Let go of your denial, let go of your fear. It is inevitable and necessary that you partake with me, Matthias. You *must* taste. You *must* see."

Always with the Matthias thing. That was the name he had coined for me while he was on The Shot, which by this point meant all the time. That's a Biblical name, by the way. Matthias replaces Judas Iscariot as the twelfth disciple. I have chosen not to read too much into that. The only reason

I even went over to Jake's place anymore was to observe him while he was high, to listen to his rants, and to try to learn something more about the users from what he had to say. I had stopped trying to convince him to stop using long before. It was a wasteful effort. The Shot instills in users an incredible conviction and willpower, not so much an addiction as a deep-seated belief in its power.

"Jake, dude, *drop it*. I am *not* interested, alright? It's not gonna happen. Do you hear yourself? Do you know how creepy you've become? How creepy *everybody* has become? Misquoting those Bible verses and talking about space and shit? It weirds me ou—"

"Matthias, *Matthias, OH!* You gentle fool. You poor, poor fool..." Jake said, putting his hands over his eyes and shaking his head. "You are blind, you are blind! You have let the scales cloud over your eyes like our brother Paul, and the only way to see clearly—to shed that wretched fish skin—is to partake in the gift with me. There is another world, a *true* world, behind this one which you do not yet see."

"Yeah, you mean the way your windows look out into space and your dining table is a stupid control panel or something? The way every cup in your goddamn cupboard is the same cup that Jesus drank out of? Is *that* how the world really is, Jake? I'll tell you: *no*, it isn't. That's just the way that green shit makes you see things that are *not really there*. You are literally losing your mind."

"No, no, Matthias," Jake said with genuine sadness. "I am gaining my mind. Just like Our Mother said, 'You must lose your mind and have the faith of a child in order to gain your true mind,' and, 'For I so loved the world that I gave The Great Gift so that whosoever should believe in it might see and know the world as through My own eyes.'"

"That is not how those passages go, Jake, not even close.

You're scrambling them all up. I can show you." I had taken up the study of the Bible in the days since The Shot and had accumulated a marginal knowledge of its content, more out of pure curiosity than truth-seeking. In fact, I surprised myself at times by the amount of passages that stuck in my memory with decent accuracy.

Jake ignored me and said, "Take it with me, Matthias. *Please*. This is the last time I will *ask* you. You have wasted enough time walking around in blindness and starvation already, and it is high time that you see. You must. You *must*, lest The Mothership comes and you, along with all the other lost, stubborn souls—those miserable deacons of *folly*—are left behind to wander the scorched earth alone."

"What does this Mothership of yours have anything to do with the Scripture you keep quoting, Jake? Have you ever thought about that? How *wacky* it sounds? What does a ship from outer space with some old broad onboard have a single thing in common with Bible verses or God or judgment? They don't even belong in the same conversation unless you're listening to some cult-following nutjob on a public access TV show! Do you think the Mothership *is* God? Is God a *woman*, as far as you're concerned, Jake? None of it makes any sense, man. Everything coming out of your mouth is contradictory and confused."

I say I had stopped trying to convince him, and yet it was hard not to argue every time I was with him. I cared about Jake. He had been a good friend before, a *great* friend, even. Any anger pouring out of me was directed at The Shot, and at his stupid decision to get hooked on it.

The tension in Jake's face eased for a moment. He looked contemplative, and in awe. "It all connects. It all connects," he said simply, as if that should be explanation enough for me. He was pulsing his hands back and forth in front of his chest, fingers arced inwards towards each other, as if there was an expanding and contracting orb between his palms. "He is The Mothership the same as She is, the same as *It* is, and they are all one. Jesus? He was a man, and a messenger, long ago, but is now the captain. The pilot on the vessel of deliverance. The Holy Ghost, he makes the ship run, like a living engine. And us, we are the children—*their* children—their sheep, their little ones, their chosen ones. We are the future crew to man the ship and guide it to Paradise, and beyond."

The smile Jake wore was so warm and authentic it would have been better suited on the face of a man meeting his newborn child for the first time, or reuniting with a long-lost lover. His eyes were dewy with tears, and he was dead-set sincere. He believed what he was saying with his whole being.

He whispered, "They come for us on the wings of the wind... and swiftly at that."

I stared at him gravely, but his eyes were far off. "I don't remember reading anything about a big fucking shiny UFO being a 'vessel of deliverance' in the Bible, Jake. Pretty sure nobody had come up with anything like that yet in the first century."

"It all connects," he sighed, as if I was a child who just wasn't getting it. "This Bible of which you speak is only one of many revelations which our Most Blessed Mother has given. Many sacred texts handed down over the centuries, and in each one are hints of Her, and of The Shot. The signs are there, Matthias, if you will only see them. The sweetest revelation of all is the voice with which She speaks to me, to each one of us, personally! Oh, Matthias, the *truths* She speaks. And She knows us each by name. It is a still, small voice, whispering things of future, present, and past unto us.

It is *wonderful.* Glorious. Divine."

Suddenly his face grew angry, and he stared me in the eyes. "*Hear* Her, Matthias," he demanded. "Listen to the words long passed down. Taste the nectar planted, grown, and harvested."

I threw my hands up, putting on a show of irritation, trying to ignore the fury in his features and how much they unnerved me. "Does The Shot impair your hearing, Jake? I am *not* doing it, man. How many times have I said that? There is no way I'm putting that shit into my body."

Instantaneously, the heat in Jake's demeanor melted and receded once more. He was a regular roller coaster ride of hellfire conviction and deep, authentic sympathy for the lost in those days—*not* the case with most users, by the way. Maybe he had an extra level of patience for me because of our history, a kindness any other user would have gladly foregone and skipped right to the violent part. Jake sighed and bowed his head, eyes closed, as if he were praying for my eternal soul. To *whom* he thought he was praying, I could only imagine. *Her*, I suppose.

Head still down, he said, "'And two men will be in the field, working the soil; one will be taken unto glory and riches and life, and the other left to scrounge and mourn and chase the wind, and ultimately… to burn in The Lake of Fire, for all truths were revealed and laid bare before him, yet still he did not believe…' Ah, the holy writ always proves so true, Matthias, although I am—for *your* sake—not glad for that fact."

He slumped down into the couch and gazed out the window like he had so many times before, his lips moving soundlessly. I knew from experience that he would remain in that state for hours on end. His Shot-inspired rant was over and he was officially gone.

I stood.

"I'm leaving, Jake. And when I walk out that door, I'm not coming back over here again," I said.

Standing in the doorway of his apartment, I turned around and said, "If you can hear me, I *really* think you should stop with this, man. I say that as a friend, or as someone who you used to consider a friend. You didn't used to be like this. That stuff is fucking with your head."

Jake kept his face pointed towards the window and pinched his eyes closed hard, as if in pain. He did not turn his head to meet my eyes.

That was the last time I saw him.

*

The internet might once have been the answer to tracking down other non-users, but by this point the web has all but dwindled to zero usability. As with consistent electricity or clean water from the tap, getting online is simply no longer a priority to people in this odd version of the world. As far as I can tell, there is no one maintaining the servers anymore (*any* of them), internet service providers no longer exist, and there is no one programming new software, hacking systems, moderating firewalls, creating viruses, generating content, blogging, tweeting, reviewing, video-diary-ing, or anything else online. Even when I could still get the occasional charge on my laptop from a salvaged battery-pack, there was no point in trying to log on because there was nowhere to go. So reaching people online is obviously out.

Moving around in the open and trying to comb through the masses on the slim possibility of finding a "normal" person among them is a surefire way to get discovered and swarmed by a mob of Shot-believers. And anyhow, other non-users (if there *are* any left) have most likely discovered the same tactics that I have and are going to be on permanent blend-in mode in public. I have failed to find any sort of underground community or meeting place for non-users, although it is not as if they can just throw up a poster ad on the community corkboard. Even two years ago when I started my wildly unsuccessful group, it was the only one of its kind that I had ever heard of, or have since. So basically, if "we" are out there, we have no way of finding each other. It's a wretched catch-22; an endless, ironic, circular curse.

Another part of me wonders, even if I found other non-users, even *one* other person, what the hell would we *do about it?* We would already be vastly outnumbered, and it's not as if even a significant group of regulars could convince the users to cease their consumption of The Shot. Even an entire army of non-users would be hard-pressed to make any sort of change at this point. The users' devotion to the substance is fully solidified. To even suggest the possibility of quitting The Shot would be madness, and invitation to be publicly martyred by way of syringe.

So, persuading the users is impossible. Stopping them by force is impossible. Altering the conviction of even one single user *might* be possible if I literally kidnapped one, strapped them to a bed, and sweated the bizarre shit out of their body until they were sober and normal again. But to what end? Even if I did something like that—and I'm not even sure that method would *work*—I would still only gain one accomplice; them and me against the world. *Then* what would we do?

Hell, what do *I* do right now? Hide out and keep scrounging for shitty, expired canned food? Keep staying in an apartment with no water or heat or light and sleeping restlessly because I'm so damn terrified that they're going to find me and stick my gut with a needle in the night? Do I just sit tight and wait this all out until the users... well, die off, if that's even *what they do?*

Shit. *Can* they die? In five years, how has this never occurred to me? Come to think of it, I have never seen a dead one, or heard of one dying. They all look so damn healthy and slim and young, like they're fixing to live forever. Even the elderly ones look like immortals. It's as if they're aging in reverse, getting younger and stronger all the time. Not a one looks anywhere close to death, judging by external appearances only.

Damn it, how has this never *occurred to me?* I mean, there was Glenn Champlain who offed himself at the beginning of all this, but that's just about the only user suicide (or death) that I can think of.

No, no... *surely* they can die, right? Of cancer or accidents or drowning or natural causes? In five years' time, plenty of people would have had to have died, wouldn't they?

Wouldn't they?

FOUR

Don't think I haven't considered using The Shot myself.

For so long, using the drug seemed to me like nothing short of madness, and most of the time it still does. But now, in Year *Six* as of last month (God, it seems hard to believe that that much time has passed), the appeal and possible benefits of using The Shot have crossed my mind many times over.

I mean, getting ahold of it would be easy. Heck, it would be *easier* than easy. Come to think of it, it would be the easiest possible thing that one could do on planet Earth at the moment, apart from breathing. Far easier than continuing to hunt and scrounge for food and water like a goddamn vulture who is rapidly running out of corpses from which to pick meat off the bones. Definitely easier than constantly hiding out like a fucking fugitive—though not from the law, but from a mass of prick-happy Bible-misquoters.

I could step outside right now, hold my arms out wide (making my body into the shape of a cross), and shout, "*I have not been enlightened! I have not been redeemed! Please, come, all you who are blessed, come and show me the way! Let me see! Let me taste! I believe, brothers and sisters, I finally believe in the perfect and pure Mothership, and in Her imminent approach!*" None of that would be true, of course, but it would sure as shit get the users' attention. They would flood to me like a beacon of light in a world of darkness.

There have been times, in moments of lonely desperation, when I have thought I was completely wrong in holding out, and that the users were actually the ones who had everything *right*. That maybe The Shot really *was* a gift to humanity, and that we were destined to take it and enjoy it (destined by whom or what, I don't know), to use it for all it is worth, and to carry on through life in zonked-out, blissfully ignorant praise until whatever came next. Mankind's bodies and minds might be purified and prepared for perfection, glory, and some version of Paradise. I've thought that maybe once every last person on Earth had given in and accepted The Shot, that *then* the world might turn over and be reborn into a new creation; all impurities washed away, every transgression forgotten, and all that has been broken would be set right. We, as a race, could begin again. Considering the other philosophies that once existed regarding humanity's fate, it's really not all that crazy an idea.

And hell, maybe there really *is* a ship.

Not a chance.

I never would have thought myself capable of such thoughts, and of such doubts about my own sanity. But when I'm the only person in a massive crowd who thinks that the emperor is parading around without his clothes on and everyone else is shouting the contrary, it can tend to mess with the faith I have in the accuracy of my own perceptions.

There have been other times—*many* times—when I've thought, "Fuck this," and found myself ready to be done with all the sneaking around, all the wondering if I'm right or wrong, all the living alone and having no one to talk to and eating shitty old food and getting so mixed up in my own head. I could just let them shoot it into my stomach and be done with all the questions and unpleasantness, all the loneliness and fear. Hand over my mind and become one of them; kick back and wait for those wonderful faux-

Biblical and Mothership thoughts to flood over me and enlighten my soul. I mean, shit—what if taking it really *did* do something good? Like in that old Spielberg movie where everyone is whistling the same little tune or seeing visions of the same piece of landscape and Richard Dreyfuss sculpts a mountain peak with his mashed potatoes. Nobody really understands why these things are happening, but then the ship comes at the end and it all makes sense and they weren't so crazy after all! The subliminal imagery was preparing them for alien arrival the whole time. Maybe The Shot only seems crazy on *this* side of the fence, but once it's in your system... who knows?

But no, goddamn it. *No...* That can't be. That *cannot* be the answer to how things play out for humanity, for how this world comes to a close. It's too batshit crazy.

It is the idea of willingly handing over of my mind that I cannot accept (as if I'm not currently losing it already), even though no user would ever phrase it that way. They would say to take The Shot was *expanding* one's mind, not losing it. They would say it is unlocking the soul, opening the eyes, freeing the spirit and all that bullshit. The thing that always holds me back from those "Fuck this" moments and keeps me grounded in the land of rationality is the fact that everyone around me is just so fucking *nuts*. Over the moon, off their rockers, toys in the attic, etc. That, and they are clearly no longer themselves. "Themselves" waved bye-bye a long time ago, and there is no diversity of personalities among people anymore, unless it is the personality made up of one collective blunder of souls speaking insanity.

It's just that... *something* has to break soon; something needs to snap and bring relief. And it's going to either be *me* or all of them. I can already tell you (though you can probably guess) which one seems more likely at the moment.

I cannot continue to live in fear, in uncertainty, in hiding. It is driving me mad. I can't trust my own thoughts half the time. So either the world is going to break loose and go to Hell in a handbag more than it already has and I will find out that *I* was the foolish one the entire time, or I am going to hold out long enough to find out that I was right all along.

*

A couple of weeks ago, I saw something horrific that I wish I could forget.

I was making my way back to my apartment with a backpack full of canned food and bottled water. I had found a "new" abandoned grocery store about seven miles away that had not yet been ransacked and still had some dusty canned inventory left in its stockroom. It was a long trek, especially having to make the journey primarily through alleyways and side roads to keep off of the streets. I noticed a commotion in the road and peeked around a corner, concealed in the alley, to see what was happening.

A group of twenty or thirty users had surrounded a young woman with strawberry blonde hair, holding arms out towards her, squeezing in too close to her face and shouting wild proclamations as they had done with me in times past.

My heart jolted in my chest. She was a *non*-user, the first I had seen in years. I could tell just by looking at her. The expression on her face, the clarity in her eyes, even from a distance.

My god! I thought, my pulse slamming through me. There *are* others like me!

My adrenaline was on overdrive, as was my mind, racing through scenarios of how I could get to her and free her from their grip, how I could save her and bring her back with me. How I might have a friend again.

What the hell was she doing out in the open? If she had survived for this long, she ought to know better.

More users were sweeping in around her (from *where?*), close to fifty of them now. They had advanced past the shouting stage. Now they took her firmly by the arms and legs, lifting her body horizontally between them. She kicked and writhed and screamed expletives at them in protest. The users forced her to the ground on her back and held her down.

I yanked at my hair and gritted my teeth. Crouched in a squatting position, I bobbed up and down, agonizing over how I could get to her, over what I could do. But what *could* I do?

Nothing, I knew. I had nothing with me for defense, and to charge into a group that large empty-handed would mean dire consequences for both of us.

One of them pulled up the woman's shirt, exposing her belly. She screamed and thrashed, her face growing red and hot with terror. An old woman emerged from the swarm and knelt down by the girl's side with a syringe full of the green shit in one hand, at the ready. The whole event was unfolding so fast and so smoothly, it was as if the users had rehearsed it. That, or they had done this very thing many times before. The old woman held the syringe out above the girl with purpose and awe, like she was about to perform a sacred tribal ritual that demanded a moment's pause before proceeding. The crowd of users had gone silent, all eyes on the girl and the old woman.

"I don't *want* it!" the girl screamed. "*Fuck all of you*

psychos, let me go! Let me go!" She kicked and thrashed wildly, but the users held fast to her limbs.

"Oh darling... My sweet, silly girl," the old woman said in a kind voice, as if she were calming a young child afraid of a great storm railing outside her bedroom window. "But you *need* it! Your eyes have not yet been opened, your frame has not yet been set free! Oh, the wonders you will see..."

Even as I watched in horror, some distant recess of my mind acknowledged an insane thought: that the girl who thrashed on the ground, surrounded by drug-addled lunatics, was cute. It was a crazy, ridiculous, typical-male thing to think, but was nonetheless true. I was—am—just so *damn lonely.* Her exposed belly was smooth and pale, like it would be exquisite to touch. Not in a sexual way, but in that the sensation of another human's bodily warmth and tenderness seemed an unutterable joy to experience. It was a sensation I had gone for so long without feeling. Her face was contorted and red by her gnashing and screaming, but in the moments before, I had recognized that her features were sweet, even kind.

A furious, protective urgency thrummed through me. I wanted to rush out from behind the corner and do some thrashing of my own, to pummel and kick and destroy those fucking users and save the girl and take her with me. Make her safe. But to reveal myself then would have meant meeting the same terrible fate.

So instead, I did all that I could do: I watched, with a horrible churn of despair writhing in the hollow of my stomach. It made me weary with sadness to think that *she* was so alone, that she didn't even know that I was there watching her only a dozen yards away, that there were others like her in the world, but we had failed to find each other in time.

Then again, maybe her not knowing was for the best.

"My sweet girl," the old woman said, "prepare to see the light!"

Even from a distance, I could see that there were tears of sincere joy in the old woman's eyes.

She plunged the syringe into the girl's stomach and emptied the tube of its sludgy green contents. The girl's body bucked upward, then tensed as she arched her back and held that position. From her throat came choked protesting noises, but they ceased as she relaxed her body to the ground. After a moment, she shook her head and blinked up at the crowd around her. Her eyes had glazed over, and I knew that any remnants of who that woman once was had vanished in the space of thirty seconds.

The users pulled her up to her feet with gentle hands and kind reassurances, as if she were rising from a baptism pool; once lost but now found, once wretched but now made clean. And glory hallelujah, she's finally seen the light.

Within moments, talk of The Mothership was already on her lips.

*

I did not think it possible for things to get any stranger, but they have.

The past few days, the sky has grown dark. And I'm not talking about any ordinary grey, overcast skies, like a regular weather system that might pass in a few days. I mean the sky *does not fucking look right*. It has morphed into a shade of bruised purple and deep red with rippling layers of gloomy, brooding grey. The whole of the sky is spread with undulating mounds of rounded dark matter that give the sensation of hanging close overhead, like a canopy tent pitched with too low of a ceiling. Any clear distinction of night and day have ceased, there is only a sickly glow that hints through the wooly clouds during the daytime hours.

It sounds foolish or crazy to say this (or perhaps it doesn't), but the sky looks to me like... *judgment.* It has the appearance of what I once would have imagined the build up to Judgment Day looking like; hellfire, brimstone, and a T-1000 sent from the future to the present to tear our shit to pieces. Ha. I just realized that I am probably the only person alive at the moment who still has any recollection what a T-1000 is. *"Have you seen this boy?"* No way in Hell a user would catch *that* reference. That seems like it ought to be a funny thought, but it isn't.

A long time ago, in college I think, I read a book called *I Am Legend* by a guy named... well, shit, his name won't come to me. He wrote another book called *Duel* and some *Twilight Zone* episodes. I don't know why I can recall *those* references, but not the author's name. Anyway, in *I Am Legend*, Robert Neville is the last man on earth (or so he thinks) who is not infected by a virus that has basically turned all of humanity into vampires. He has to hide out to survive and his resources are limited, but he makes things work. The world he once knew is long gone, and for much of the novel Neville is slowly going mad with loneliness and despair (not to mention self-medicating with copious amounts of whiskey). Minus the alcohol part, I can't help but be reminded of that story now and resonate with how Robert Neville—albeit a fictional man—must have felt.

One big difference: he had a dog. For a time, anyway. Despite all the apocalyptic end-of-the-world bloodthirsty-populous bullshit he was enduring, at least he had a companion to keep him occupied. The dog in the book was a stray, and was too afraid to come right up to Neville for a long while. He has to lure the dog closer and closer, day by day, for *weeks*, but even the daily anticipation of that small, distant connection is enough to keep Neville going. Enough to give him hope, to give him something to look forward to.

God, what I would give for a friend right now. Even one who couldn't talk. There *aren't* any dogs left, by the way, so that particular scenario is out of the question for me. Dogs, cats, birds, and every other commonly seen animal disappeared around the time babies stopped showing up back in Year Two or so.

I am honestly not sure what happened to all the animals. It was like they slowly faded out of existence, so slowly and discreetly that nobody noticed until they were completely gone. Maybe the animals could sense instinctually that something had gone sour in the world and they all migrated away, even the ones that do not, by nature, migrate. Or maybe they just walked and walked in one direction until they hit the ocean and just kept walking into it until they were consumed. The birds might have flown south, although I'm not sure where they would go that would be any different from anywhere else because The Shot is in the south, too.

Anyway, Robert Neville's story does not end well. The dog becomes infected, and while he tries desperately to save his friend and nurse him back to health, there is nothing he can do to stop the virus from ravaging the dog's body. It is not an easy scene to read when the dog is moaning and convulsing in Robert's arms, making a painful transition from canine into something horrible.

This defeat—heaped upon the many *other* defeats Neville had already experienced—is enough to nearly make his mind snap. From the beginning of the story, it is clear that Neville is a resilient man, not easily broken. But I guess even the toughest, most hardened men can still be worn down by loneliness, loss, and most of all, time.

That is what troubles me now. I am *not* like Robert Neville. I am not tough, or hardened, resourceful or strong. I am not special. In a movie about this sort of situation, I would not be the most likely candidate to have survived for this long. As far as I can figure, I am only alive and Shot-free because I've just been lucky enough to not get caught.

THREE

Jesus, they *found me*.

They came in the middle of the night, something like thirty users, and broke into my third-floor apartment, despite the steel brace and heavy padlock I had installed across the door. My apartment was nowhere near any of their gathering places (that I knew of), and the entire rest of my building was empty. But somehow they still found me.

Maybe their senses are growing stronger, and they can actually *smell* a non-user from afar by way of some Shot-fueled instinct. Maybe they've developed new senses that allow them to find non-users like me. But then, why would they send only thirty users to fetch me when there are surely *droves* of the faithful? Maybe it was only a scouting team, if they are even cognitively aware enough to organize such a thing. Still—greater sensory awareness or not—they did not have enough good sense to climb the three flights of stairs to my apartment more quietly. They thumped and crowded in the stairwell, banging against the walls in the landings, so I felt and heard a rumble building from the floors below.

I was awake before they reached me. I poked my head into the living room in time to see my front door being splintered to pieces and the hollow grind of screws ripping out of the drywall. In seconds, they had broken through the door and were flooding into the living room, many of them with syringes at the ready, needles bared, loaded with green and prepped to inject.

"We have found you brother, *sing praises!*" one of them said. The others were calling out their own variations of the same:

"Fear not, we bring peace!"

"Taste the nectar of life eternal!"

"*PARTAKE!*"

I receded back into the bedroom and tried to slam the door shut, but they were already coming through it. I threw open the bedroom window and flung myself out onto the fire escape with them right on my tail. Their needles aimed jabs through the air to find purchase in my skin while their free hands swiped to snag at my clothes. I began a rapid, jerky descent down the rickety steel stairs.

The users began to pour out of the window after me, flipping and tumbling over each other onto their backs or bellies like newborn serpents rolling out of their mother's hot, wet womb. A few of them made it out, but too many bodies shoved at once and they got jammed up in the window frame.

Like a *Three Stooges* gag, I thought, wildly. The ol' stuck-in-the-window frame bit.

This did not stop the clogged-up users from shouting their riotous proclamations at me as I ran, pleading that I would let them open my eyes.

The users who had gotten onto the fire escape chased after me; some, on their feet; others, on their stomachs, clutching with hooked fingers into the webbed-steel grating of the steps to scrape themselves forward and down. Those on their feet clanged steadily down the steps and were at my heels by the time I reached the last set of stairs.

I had been so busy just getting down the fire escape that I had failed to notice that there were another seven or eight users crowded loosely around the base of the steps, staring up at me with blank faces. They watched my rapid approach dumbly, as if taken by surprise and unsure what they would do when I reached them. My imagination came up with the wild picture of a cluster of slack-jawed bowling pins awaiting the tumultuous crash of a strike. I would be the bowling ball in that scenario.

I was really moving by this point and had the downward momentum on my side, so I tucked in my right arm and slammed my right shoulder into the crowd, bursting through their barricade like a defensive lineman and knocking a handful of them to the ground. I thought I was home-free when I was yanked violently backward.

One of them had clamped their hands firmly onto my left arm, and another that I had shoved to the ground snagged hold of my right leg. For a terrifying split second I nearly lost my balance and toppled down for good. I kicked with my free leg and thrashed with my free arm, keeping my eyes ahead towards open space and freedom.

In that moment, a film reel flashed through my head of every nightmare I had ever dreamt. Dreams where some wretched thing in the dark had me in a death-grip, my mind pleading with my body to *run*, but my limbs would not move correctly, too slow like trying to sprint underwater. Dreams where I would find myself in a familiar room in the house of my childhood, but some deeply felt sense of evil and dread filled the corners. Then the lights click off and a door would slam shut, leaving me in darkness and awaiting some unseen wicked thing. I would know I was dreaming but *could not* wake up. Dreams I had as a kid where I was running from a shadowy bad man in my closet or a ventriloquist dummy come to life with murderous intentions, and in the dream I would run up to my parents, pulling at their pant-legs and screaming for them to help, to notice me, to pick me up and save me, but they couldn't see me, were deaf to hear me, and were blind to me being swallowed alive.

Caught in the users' grip, I felt the same writhing dread in the pit of my stomach, and the accompanying thought *can I please please please wake up now?* But it was no dream (a nightmare, yes), and I was *not* about to let myself be swallowed alive.

I felt more hands and fingertips snatching at my back, clutching hold of the fabric of my jacket. I managed to kick my leg free from the user on the ground, so I took advantage of this small freedom and swung my right fist with every ounce of weight that I could load into it and smashed the face of the user who held my left arm.

In the split second before my fist connected with his face, my adrenaline-hyped mind recognized—crazily and in slow-motion—that this dead-eyed user who had latched onto my arm actually looked like he would have been a nice guy before The Shot took over his system. In his thirties, balding, a thin face with round wire-rimmed glasses and a well-groomed mustache. Very teacher-y, the kind who might have been glad to give you an extra day to finish a paper, or stay after class with you discussing a good book that you had both read. But those eyes... Crazed and open too wide, which reminded me that he was just another user. Whatever man he had once been was now long gone.

So I knocked the shit out of him.

His head cracked to the side and blood flew from his nose, but he didn't go down. Still, my purpose was served: the punch had distracted him momentarily and I yanked my arm free. I had enough forward momentum to writhe free from the other users clutching my clothes.

My body freed, I ran like hell itself was on my heels. I guess it pretty much was.

*

I ran for a long time. Too long. I knew it wasn't good to be exposed for so long in the open, but I didn't have much of a choice. It had been around three in the morning when the mob of users had swarmed my apartment, and I was still running when the sun peaked orange over the horizon. I was running still when it was full in the sky.

Before I reached the edge of the city, a handful of users wandering about in the early morning had spotted me and began their own half-hearted pursuits, but I outran them all. The users are *jogging* now—more than they used to do—but still cannot quite seem to full-out sprint, or are simply not interested enough to do so.

My lungs felt torn and scorched inside my chest by the time I finally slowed to a flailing jog, then to a stumbling walk, on the outskirts of town. I collapsed to my knees and hunched over while sucking in great gulps of breath, head hanging and fists on the asphalt, trying to calm my system back down. My heart whammed in an unsteady rhythm, and I was briefly terrified that I might be having a heart attack. *No, too young for that*, I thought. *Aren't I?* I forced myself to concentrate on breathing slowly and deeply until my pulse finally slowed, but I was still gasping for at least another twenty minutes.

Eventually, I stood up. The landscape on either side of the road was green with swaying tall grasses over expansive rolling fields, flush with weeds grown rampant, and spotted with wide, burly trees. The road itself was cracked and sun-beaten, long past its last repaving. The once-black asphalt had faded to a crumbly pale grey with dry bursts of tanned yellow grass reaching between the cracks. Ahead and to my left another ninety yards or so further up the highway was a disheveled barn of warped planks and flaking red paint the color of cheap country wine.

On shaking legs, I ambled slowly towards the barn. It sat on what looked to have been a pretty nice farm at one time. Two small wooden buildings situated nearby the barn had collapsed into untidy heaps of boards and rafters. Among the ruins of one of these, I saw what looked like a small church steeple jagging up and out at a wild diagonal angle. If it ever was a church, or a chapel, it couldn't have been any bigger than a two-car garage. Everything on the property was wildly overgrown (including a horse corral crowded with vegetation taller than the wood-post fence that surrounded it), and the weeds and wild grass had long since choked out whatever crop used to grow across the many fields—who would maintain what nobody eats anymore? However, remnants of the sowing lines were still visible through all the tangled green.

I had reached the barn, but before going inside, I turned around and let my eyes slowly scan the horizon, searching for any minute sign of movement along the road or in the tall grass. After several minutes, I could find no cause for alarm. Satisfied (mostly) that no users had seen or pursued me, I slid open the great creaking door of the barn on its rusty track and stepped inside.

It was pitch-black, save for a few flickering hints of sunlight poking through various cracks in the siding and a jagged hole in the roof. The floor was hard-packed dust scattered with dry sprigs of hay, and the whole place smelled musty and long out of use. The tangy scent of ancient animal piss and sour shit still hung thick on the air. Once my eyes had adjusted to the dim light, I could make out an open loft at the back of the barn, about ten or twelve feet off the ground, and an old wooden ladder leaned against its edge.

I shuffled towards the ladder, intent on checking out the loft and seeing if it was fit for a place to rest for a while. My feet were aching and numb, and my legs trembled so badly they threatened to give out beneath me. I put a foot on the bottom rung when a thought occurred to me.

The door.

I went to the rear wall of the barn and felt around in the dark for something heavy to push in front of the door. There was an enormous tractor tire propped in one corner. It was heavy as shit and almost as tall as me, but I was able to shimmy it away from the back wall and roll it across the dusty floor. I positioned it parallel to the sliding barn door and tipped it over diagonally to lean its weight against the handle. I thought of the Roman soldiers who sealed Jesus' tomb with a big round stone, only in reverse, as if the tomb had been sealed up from the inside.

I quickly shooed that comparison out of my head because, after all, it was a *tomb* those Romans had been sealing. I didn't like thinking about the possibility of the barn being mine.

With the tire in place, I lumbered gently on sore feet across the room to the ladder. The wooden rungs felt thin in my hands and the whole ladder quivered under my weight. I pulled myself into the loft and was relieved to find large piles of old hay. Moldy and full of mice, probably, but to me it looked as welcoming and cozy as a brand new mattress.

I collapsed into the pile, causing a considerable plume of dust and debris to dance into the air. I was seconds away from sleep when a gracious spark of wisdom hit me from some unknown place. I managed to get up from the hay bed and pulled the ladder up into the loft with me, effectively securing myself one step further, high out of reach should any users make their way through the door.

I flopped myself back down and almost fell asleep again, but realized I was completely parched… and had no water. I had no *anything*, in fact. All of my supplies, my food, my clothes and few belongings were back at the apartment. The apartment that I could not ever risk returning to. In the rush of just getting the hell out of there, I had forgotten to grab anything important.

Shit.

Well, thirsty I could handle, for a little while, until I got some rest. I was too tired to worry about the rest.

I dropped deeply into sleep and dreamt only of unpleasant things.

*

It had been three days since I found the barn, and I was *so fucking hungry*. My stomach had been churning and making deep, angry grumbles for about eighteen hours straight.

Water was, thankfully, not a problem to find. There was an old-fashioned well with stone siding and a bucket on a rope and crank. I could not see to the bottom of the well, but there was a plentiful supply. The water had a bit of an earthy, mineral taste, but it was cold and very refreshing.

In lieu of food, I tried gorging myself on water, chugging it until I couldn't hold any more to trick my stomach into thinking it was full for a little while. That just made me waddle around with a sloshy, sore gut for a few minutes before spewing the clear liquid back up.

During the day, I scoured the fields and all over the grounds for anything edible; an old dried-up head of corn, wild strawberries, carrots or potatoes or something, but no luck. Everything good seemed to have been strangled out by the weeds and grass.

There was an old farmhouse on the property that leaned *horribly* to one side and looked ready to collapse at any moment. I searched inside it too—cautiously and as fast as I could while it groaned and creaked around me—but it was as hollow and useless as everything else on the farm. Every window had been broken out and there were remnants of charred furniture in the fireplace. The cabinets and pantry were stocked with nothing but spiderwebs and dust. I suspect that it had been abandoned even before the days of The Shot.

I tried eating some grass, but it was stringy, mud-tasting, and impossible to swallow without gagging. Even in my intense hunger, my throat refused to take it down. I remembered hearing something a long time ago that yellow dandelion heads were edible. Turns out they are, and in fact they don't taste too bad, but I could only find a few of them.

In the tall grass, I tripped over part of a moldy wooden sign lying face down. It had been covered over and tangled in the brush for a long time. It was curved in an arch shape but had been broken approximately in the middle. I leaned it up and brushed off the damp soil from its face. In ugly hand-carved letters, I could make out *ING POST RANCH*. The other half of the sign was nowhere nearby that I could find. Maybe it had been swallowed up by the brush.

The *ING POST RANCH*, I thought. My new temporary home. Lovely. Well, *ING POST*, did anyone ever fucking eat anything around here?

I found a moldy burlap sack of cornmeal in a corner of the barn. I ripped it open and scooped up a handful to sample, but it was like eating sand pebbles mixed with manure. It sucked all the moisture out of my mouth, turning it into a dry, wheezing cavity. The stuff was clearly years and years old, and even fresh, I don't know if it would have been edible by itself.

I would have just killed an animal—*any* animal—and roasted the shit out of it to have a veritable feast, if I could have only found one. The wild creatures must have gone bye-bye along with all the dogs and cats a few years back.

Anyway, I knew that I *had* to find something to eat, and soon. I was shaky, tense, had a constant headache, and got random bouts of irritation that graduated to irrational rage. I knew that my thoughts were not as sharp as they should have been. And they *needed* to be if I wanted to stay alive.

In a world that was no longer interested in producing sustenance for humans, it was hard enough finding something to eat while living in the city, but out in the middle of nowhere there was absolutely *piddly-shit*. I suppose that, given long enough, I could have salvaged some seeds from the field or found something to cultivate and grow, but I didn't exactly have until harvest time to wait around for a fucking green bean.

There was a pitchfork that I found in the barn; three-pronged, devil-like. It was a little rusty, but the tines were plenty sharp, and it was lightweight, easy to handle. It was about the best thing I had found so far that could serve as a weapon, should that be necessary.

I went to bed in the barn on that third night at the farm, committed to the idea that in the morning I was going to grab that pitchfork, walk boldly back into town, and get myself something *to fucking eat.*

*

In the golden light of the early morning, I walked in the direction of the city I had been running from only three days earlier.

I came upon an old convenience store and gas station that looked long forgotten. Its windows and storefront were dirty, and the parking lot was overgrown with weeds, but otherwise the establishment seemed like it had been left alone. The double glass doors were not locked.

I swung the left one open and went inside. A bell dinged above my head as I crossed the threshold—an actual bell, not some electronic substitute. After that was nothing but quiet, dimness, and dust. Vague bluish light came in through the store's tinted front windows, but the place was mostly dark since the fluorescent fixtures overhead were not lit. Even in the dim light, the vibrant purple and green advertisements for The Shot were everywhere throughout the store; glossy signs twirling on strings dangling from the ceiling, tall folded cardboard displays interrupting the open areas, colorful announcements sticking up from the tops of shelves. As if The Shot needed any promotional propaganda to move units. From the place I stood, every white metal rack was completely empty but for the ghost rings in dust of the product it once held.

In the convenience store's final days—before its Shot-addled store owners closed up shop for good and decided to permanently join their Shot-addled friends in some massive arena for ongoing corporate praise, no doubt—The Shot had probably been their primary (or only) inventory, but that did not stop me from scouring every aisle, rack, and drink cooler in the place for something preserved and edible.

It occurred to me that any establishment carrying The Shot *going out of business* was an odd and unlikely scenario.

But perhaps the location was too far out of the way, and most users had a closer source.

The back wall of the store was lined with wide glass-doored cooler cases that would have once held frosty cold sodas, beer, and ice, but that stock had probably also been replaced with The Shot at some point. One cooler in the far corner, though not running any longer, was partially stocked with dusty bottles of purified water. I was grateful for the discovery and made a mental note to take all I could back with me, but water was not my priority.

As if body agreed with mind (and right on cue), my stomach gave a deep, wet grumble.

From the corner of my eye, on the bottom tier of a shelf in the rear of the store, I caught glimpse of a few metal cans and plastic containers. I practically dove towards them and snatched up the closest item to me: a small white plastic bowl with a red lid. It was a container of Chef Boyardee Cheese Ravioli in Tomato & Meat Sauce.

Shit, I hadn't seen one of them in ages. A memory hit me then of taking these very same containers in a blue hot-or-cold plush zippered lunch bag (with my first and last name Sharpied on the top) to elementary school, of heating them up in a dirty cafeteria microwave, of thinking at the time that they were one of the greatest lunches ever invented, topped only by the Lunchables make-your-own-pizza combos that came with a little miniature candy bar.

Better times, a simpler life.

I flipped over the Chef Boyardee package in my hand, more out of habit than actually caring what I would find. The expiration date stamped in black blocky letters on the bottom of the bowl was more than four years past, which meant it had probably been manufactured something like five or six years back. But I have long since been convinced that expiration dates were merely legal requirements to save food companies' asses from food-poisoning lawsuits. Things like that don't mean shit in times like this.

Slumped against the back wall of the convenience store, I popped off the red lid, tossed aside the tiny flat "spoon" the good folks at ConAgra Foods had included in the package, ripped off the shiny silver vacuum seal, and gulped down the chunky red mixture in only a few chomps. Sure, the cheese wrapped in the ravioli tasted a little off—too tangy, maybe—but the texture was just like I remembered, and the pasta sauce tasted good as new.

On the dusty white bottom shelf there were three more raviolis, one tub of Spaghetti & Meatballs in Tomato Sauce, two cans of Hormel Beef Chili (*with Beans!*), and five cans of Green Giant creamed corn—sufficient sustenance for three days or more. I was wiping my mouth with the back of my sleeve and reaching for another bowl of the Chef when I heard the gritty sound of sliding dust on the floor as the front door was pulled open.

The bell that once cheerfully rang to announce a new customer strolling in dinged again as I heard the one-two crunch of a pair of shoes stepping inside. I froze and held my breath.

I was crouched low at the back of the store, and the rows of shelves were blocking my view of who had come in. Not as if *who* it was required much explanation. My heart was whamming in my chest. Blood pounded through my ears in great rushes. My pulse seemed so loud I was fearful it would give me away.

Whoever had come in was hesitating—or listening. They were just standing there inside the entrance with the door held open, waiting. They must have been breathing softly because I did not hear even the faintest sound. I held my breath.

A man's soft, sincere voice cut through the silence. "Brother, have you, too, seen the light?"

Fuck.

The first reaction that occurred to me (though, in hindsight, not the wisest one) was to jolt up to my feet and call out, "Yes, brother!" across the aisles to the shadowy figure standing in the doorway. It came out way too enthusiastic and my voice was quivering terribly. "The b-blessed Mothership! Oh, how long m-must we wait for it's—eh—her return!"

The user only stared at me for a moment. The light was coming in from behind him, so his features were dark and obscure. Then he answered, "Indeed, how long..." There was suspicion in his tone, a characteristic I had not realized users were capable of having.

A beat, then he asked, "What are you doing here, friend? So far from the others, and crawling around on the floor of this place?"

My heart was slamming, my mind scratching for a response. No other time in my life have I fainted, but at that moment I felt horribly close to doing so. I hoped that the user could not make out the gleam of sweat on my forehead. I committed every ounce of my will to maintaining a blank, normal countenance, like one of them.

"I-I... have traveled from another city. Brother. And I sought shelter here. I longed to see... um. To meet other brothers and sisters of the faith, and to share, uh, joy in anticipation with them. Glory!"

The last word came out all wrong; forced and unnecessary, laying it on too thick.

I chanced a look out the window and saw fifteen to twenty *more* users standing outside the entrance with curious faces. Some of them were cupping their hands to peer in the windows. The guy talking with me may have been a scout, and the others were all waiting on his report.

I realized then that the store probably had not been abandoned by happenstance.

A trap, I thought. That's why there was still food left on the shelves. Strategically placed, maybe. Are users even mentally capable of coming up with a thing like that? Would they go to the trouble?

Yes, I thought. I believe they would.

Things had been silent for too long. The user in the doorway's face had not changed, nor had he moved from his spot.

Finally, he lifted a hand, held it out to me, and said, "Well then, come, brother. Come into our fold and be blessed. You have many friends here. We will partake in The Great Gift together and, as you say, wait in glorious anticipation until the Mother finally comes."

I stayed where I was, and thought suddenly of the three-tined pitchfork I had brought with me from the barn for defense. A lot of good it would do me now. It was leaning against the wall just inside the door—within reach of the user, ironically enough—where I had placed it while I scoped the place out.

Idiot.

I thought about the possibility of racing for the back of the store, taking my chances that I could find the rear exit and escape. But bolting would immediately give me away, and if the place *was* a setup, the users had most likely barred the rear door, or had more of their number stationed there. If I could keep them convinced that I was one of their own at least until I was back outside, I figured that I would be more likely to get an opportunity for a clean sprint away.

Resolved that it was my only option, I shuffled slowly towards the front of the convenience store. Now *all* of the users outside had their faces smashed against the window, eyes wide and dumb and fascinated. The user in the doorway still held out his open hand. I closed mine over his and did my best to subdue the shiver that rang through me. His hand was clammy, cold, and dead, like gripping a moist, blood-grimed animal skin wrapped around an ice-block.

I could see his eyes now. Arctic blue rings with too-large, too-black pupils. Vacant and lifeless, like all the others. These horrific doll's eyes had locked onto mine and I found I could not look away, though I wanted to more than anything.

The man led me by the hand out the door and onto the parking lot. I dragged my feet and scraped them across the floor, moving along to this destination as slowly as he would allow. The other users all swirled in around me and gazed like I was some incredible artifact that had just been unearthed. They leaned in too close and their breath on me was stale, like the air in a crypt.

"Hello, uh, friends," I said, and nodded to them. "The b-blessed Mothership, and um… amen."

Keep your shit together. You're losing it.

The first user still had my hand, though I had gently tried to drop it from his grip.

"Here," an elderly woman in the crowd said, "have some of mine, son." She produced an expensive-looking soft-leather case and unzipped it ceremoniously. Inside was a neat row of five glass syringes tucked beneath a thin elastic band, each of them brimming with the shiny green slime. The woman unsheathed one needle and positioned the shaft between the index and forefinger of her right hand. With her left, she reached out and lifted up the front of my shirt.

The violation of her unashamed touch made my guts swim with nausea and my skin prickle with tingling gooseflesh. I lurched back from the coldness of her hand on my stomach, my mind racing, snatching, clawing for a solution, for a way out of this.

A few of the users circled around the old woman and I were leaning in and panting aloud, their pink tongues dangling out of their mouths. They rubbed their hands together in anticipation.

The man who had come into the store still held one of my hands in both of his.

"I—I, uh, I have had plenty enough of the green nectar, good sister. I have drunk my fill for today, you might say, and m-my thoughts are... quite enlightened."

The old woman gazed right into me, through me, *beyond* me. She wore a look of pity and conviction. "There is... always room for more, young brother," she said. It came out confused, like a question.

A pause. Her eyes flicked away from mine, then back.

Her right hand shot forward like a viper strike and I felt a sharp prick of pain as the needle bit into my gut.

I lunged backwards, simultaneously planting a foot in the woman's midsection to shove her away. The old bitch was more solid than she should have been—than she could have *possibly* been for her size and frail age, yet she did not fall or even stumble. It was akin to kicking a cinderblock wall. Still, my purpose was served. The syringe in her hand had not yet been emptied of its wretched contents, and had in fact been jerked back out of my body. In the slow-motion madness of the moment, I saw a bead of my own blood hanging from the needle's tip in the woman's hand.

Thrown off-balance, my back and shoulders slammed into bodies behind me, and I yanked my hand out of the man's grasp. I began swinging my arms frantically, gnashing my teeth at them and connecting with flesh wherever I could.

These users were *much* stronger than any I had ever encountered before, even the ones I broke free from four days earlier when they invaded my apartment. These users were wholly unaffected by my blows, and I could feel the strength in their grip as they rushed around me, snatching at my limbs. I envisioned—the mad thoughts of a man close to death—a mud-and-blood game of rugby, all shoulders and hustle and combined momentum, where I was on one team, and *all of them* were on the other.

"Do not fight it, brother," one user said from the crowd.

"There is no need to be afraid," said another, gently.

"Enlightenment is so near, young one. You need only receive to it, to let it take over."

Their voices were soothing, welcoming. Unfitting for the circumstances.

I was enmeshed in a pulsing mass of bodies. Each of my limbs were held firmly, as if in iron stocks, by more than one set of impossibly strong hands. I felt my feet leave the ground as the users lifted my body, face down, into a horizontal position in their hands, just as I had watched them lift the pretty blonde girl not so long before.

I thrashed my limbs against them (*just like the girl had*), but to no avail. They rolled me in their hands to face upwards, delicately, like I was a prize pig roasting over flames on a slow-turning spit. All of their pasty faces with smiles like skull's grins hovered above me. I could not stand to see their dead, vacant eyes any longer, so I shut mine tight. I stopped fighting.

Some icy hand lifted my shirt, and I felt the poke of a needle enter my flesh.

A whipcrack rang through the air, and my eyes snapped open.

A user on the outer ring of the huddle around me crumpled to the ground, making almost no sound as his body folded limply to the pavement. Still held horizontal by many hands, I craned my neck and could see through a forest of legs that the user who had just gone down had a red, wet hole in his forehead.

All was still for a moment. All was silent, but for the users' heavy breathing.

The users had raised their heads and were peering every which way, trying to locate the source of the gunshot. I lifted my head to look at my stomach and the needle was still pierced there, standing erect on its own, although the green substance remained in its glass cage.

Another sharp crack ripped through the air. A second user went down, a woman. She collapsed sideways and this time I heard the ugly smack of her head bouncing once off the pavement.

This second execution set half of the users immediately into motion towards the sound. The others stayed behind and held on to me. They had momentarily forgotten all about giving me the injection.

The scouting users were headed towards a series of low buildings across the street from the gas station; a row of simple country storefronts, most of them with blown out windows revealing shadowy, cavernous insides. Whoever was doing the killing was presumably tucked away in those shadows, remaining out of sight.

"Please. Stop," said one of the users shuffling towards the gunshots. "Thou shalt not kill, sweet brother or sister. There is no need! Hatred has ceased, redemption draws near."

Even with their lives being directly threatened, the users were trying to convert non-believers—a murderous one, in this case—to the bitter end.

Their voices called out to the shooter, still unseen.

"Please, The Mothership, you must be patient until we see her. You must taste of the sweet gift!"

"When She comes, death will be no longer! Every tear will be wiped away. There is no need for your anger and fear!"

"There is always room in Her blessed fold for the doubting and the damned. Only, see *now*, friend, before it is *too late!*"

An elderly man at the front of the pack was holding out a readied syringe in a trembling hand as he walked in the direction of the shots.

"Please, child," he said. "Take some of mine!"

In response to that last, from way off in the distance, came another voice. Though extremely faint, I could make out the words just fine.

"There *is* no Mothership, you fuckin' loonies. But *please*, have some of *mine*."

Three more shots boomed through the air in rapid succession, and each one connected with a user's head, their bodies flailing to the ground like linens whipped off of a clothesline by the wind.

I squinted my eyes at the open window from which the gunfire seemed to be coming, but could make out nothing but darkness.

The users holding me were getting fidgety, darting their eyes from each other, to me, to their quickly dying friends, back to each other. They had clearly never encountered such violent opposition before, and were uncertain what to do with the situation. It was amazing to witness, in some terrible way; real fear was the most authentic human reaction I had ever seen poke through the emotion-numbing effects of The Shot.

The users sent scouting across the street had almost reached the building. They were moving in a quick, lopsided shamble, the closest thing to a run I had ever seen them do. The whole pack had syringes in hand now, twitching them nervously in front of themselves, stabbing at ghosts, the tiny silver needles their only hope of defense.

Just before they reached the entrance, something happened so quickly that at first I was not certain I had really seen it: from one of the shadowy open doorways on the strip of old storefronts, I could *just* make out the flash of a hand flicking out into the open, close to the ground, then sucking back into the pall, like the in-out flicker of a snake's tongue. A small, lumpy grey object tumbled happily from its grip, rolling to a stop in the middle of the crowd of scouts.

The first association that entered my head was that the hand had just thrown a grounder. But the object rolling into the middle of the users was no baseball.

An incredible blast went off in a great flash of yellow-white fire, and the users in front of the shop were flung askew with limbs flailing like rubber-bands, their green-filled syringes twirling out of their hands in slow-motion somersaults. The lot of them landed in untidy heaps of gore on the pavement. Burns and blood covered their mangled bodies. A few faces were gone completely, only glistening pink and red lumps left in their places.

A thick black smoke hung in the air and rolled upward from the ground, obscuring the door behind it. A figure stepped through the smoke, clad in all black and gripping a sizable gun that hung on a shoulder sling. The figure walked calmly and methodically to each of the fallen users and proceeded to pop off several rounds into their heads, confirming the kills.

The figure then raised its head toward myself and the users still holding me. It began to make swift, confident strides in our direction, gun angled smugly upward on its shoulder.

The users holding me had been watching this scene unfold with as much terror and fascination as I. The figure's rapid approach broke their spell. Above me, a male user made eye contact with the old woman across from him—the same who had stuck me with the needle and whom I had kicked away. The man nodded to her, and for a moment I thought they were agreeing to chase after the executioner in the same suicidal fashion as their dead friends.

Instead, the woman gripped the syringe still sticking out of my stomach and jammed her thumb down on the plunger. I watched the green shit I had fought so hard to stay away from finally make its triumphant invasion into my body.

The deed done, the users dropped me and ran. I fell to the pavement on my back and got the wind knocked out of me, my head clopping smartly against the blacktop.

Things did not go black, but they might as well have.

TWO

I woke up in darkness.

I found myself lying on what felt like a *real*, cushy, comfortable mattress, complete with fresh sheets beneath me and a warm comforter on top. It had been a long time since I had slept on something so nice. I lifted my head, but the room (though I could not see it) spun like crazy; a sensation similar to being drunk, dizzy, and sea sick all at once. My stomach lurched, threatening to vacate its meager contents of Chef Boyardee. I laid still and controlled my breathing until the waves in my head and belly calmed. I was extremely groggy and felt as if I could have just gone on sleeping forever, yet once I was awake, I felt compelled to stay that way.

My mind posed the typical questions: *Where am I? How did I get here? Where is here? Did the users bring me to one of their communes?*

The darkness was disorienting, so pitch black that I could not discern any corners of the room, a door, or even a window. I forced myself to sit up—a considerable effort—and felt around for the edge of the bed. I swung my legs down and sat on the side, blinking and staring wide-eyed into the full black, willing my vision to adjust enough to see any dim shape around me.

I replayed the last event that I could remember: that woman had stuck me with The Shot—

Holy shit, I thought, my heart fluttering. They gave me The Shot. That shit was in me. *Is* in me.

But... at the moment I felt no effect. I did not *feel* high,

I felt like *me*. Other than the grogginess, my head seemed clear and like itself. My thoughts were my own; no Scripture quoting or visions of the Mothership. I searched my memory for anything after the moment I was given the injection, but came up with nothing. I remembered being held above the ground by the users and seeing that figure approaching us with a giant gun over its shoulder.

That figure...

A door opened at a corner of the room, and a dim wash of light encased the silhouette of a person.

A woman's voice said: "How's your head? Little fuzzy, I'll bet."

I realized that my head was not the only thing that was fuzzy. Even with the new light in the room, my eyes refused to focus on her. I squinted, but everything was blurred at the edges, like looking through tears.

I answered her in an uncontrolled slur. "Iss-s ohlkay." My tongue was dry and felt long out of practice. I smacked my mouth and tasted the sour musk of unbrushed teeth and long sleep.

She approached me with one item in each hand and sat on the bed beside me, close. The mattress sank slightly under her weight, and I could smell the faint, wonderful scent of her; a clean, floral fragrance, maybe from a shampoo, mixed with a hint of honey or cherry lip balm, and beneath that a more masculine—though not unpleasant—scent like gun cleaning oil, and maybe sawdust. I had not been physically near enough to another person (a non-user, anyway) to appreciate their scent in so long.

I smelled something else, too. A rich, impossible smell that I had not encountered in years: freshly brewed coffee.

"Drink this first, you're dehydrated," she said, handing me a sealed bottle of water. "Then this. It'll help clear your head." She held out the mug of coffee, steam swirling up out of its brim.

I wanted to chug them both at once. Instead, I cracked open the bottle of water and downed it in a few long gulps; it was cold and wet and refreshing, like sipping from a clear, cool stream. The coolness ran through me and settled into my empty stomach, giving me a brief, shivering thrum of goosebumps. I set the empty bottle aside and told her thanks. She passed me the coffee. I sipped cautiously off the top, testing the heat. It was bold and piping hot and wonderful, and I could taste a hint of something mildly spicy and sweet underneath. Rum.

While I sipped, she said, "I gave you a pretty heavy tranquilizer to overpower The Shot, or at least to knock you the fuck out until it wore off. You've been out cold for sixteen hours or so. You have any dreams of spaceships or Jesus or anything?"

My head was quickly blooming back into clarity. The coffee was doing its job of perking me up, and quick. The rum, on the other hand, was just nice to have around. "Not... not that I remember."

I noticed that the mug I was holding had a scratched and faded decal of Garfield on it—old Garfield, eighties-era Garfield, from the early days of the comic strips when he was *really* fat. He wore a huge, mischievous grin, and above his head was a word bubble that said, "Never trust a smiling cat."

"Good," she said. "But don't be surprised if you find yourself blabbing some convoluted Scripture or having a false memory of being inside a space station over the next couple of hours. Even though the direct high only lasts a while from one use, that shit is still in your system. First time you've taken it? Er—had it given to you, that is?"

I nodded slowly, gazing a thousand yards in front of me, through the wall and into nothingness.

"I figured," she said. "I tried it once myself back in the early days, back when people were just fooling around with it, not making it the fucking end-all be-all of their entire lives, so I know how long the effects can stick around. The high was kinda interesting at first, but I got freaked out about what it did to me. I didn't like the thoughts I had, you know? Not feeling in control of myself, and seeing all that futuristic *Star Trek* shit in the real world where it didn't belong. Shiny silver furniture and fucking control panels with blinking lights set into the walls. Those hallucinations were *way* too real on the green shit, convincing me that *that* was my reality and not the other way around. No wonder people want to be on it all the time. So, I wised up early and swore off it for good." She paused, then added, "I think history has proven that that was a pretty fuckin' good call." She shrugged. "Or maybe not, considering where we are."

"I haven't heard of many people—well, *anyone* actually—trying The Shot only a few times and choosing to stay off it. Seems like it was addiction at first taste for the rest of the world."

"I don't know why I'm any different than the rest of them," she said. "For all I know, I should be out there babbling and praising along with them, higher than Hunter Thompson and iron-clad addicted. But when I used The Shot, I went into the experience with pretty open eyes; I tried to remain very self aware. I toyed around with lots of drugs in those days, but always with caution. I wanted to have a good time, not become a junky. Except using The Shot didn't feel like getting high, it felt like peeking behind a curtain to the dark and living things that run behind the world, just beyond our consciousness. Freaked me the fuck out, so that was it for me. Clearly, not many others share my feelings towards the stuff."

I nodded. "So... those users that stuck me, did they run off?"

"I killed them," she said flatly. "That's all you can do anymore. We're past the point of convincing any of them to stop using or to listen to reason. And they weren't about to just let me walk off with you over my shoulder without circling back around and stabbing *me* with a needle, so I chased them down and shot them each in the head. It's not like they're exactly fast on their feet. I saw your pitchfork, by the way. Cute weapon." She laughed, although not cruelly.

I had to grin despite myself. The thought of a hay-bailing tool against an army of drug-addled madmen seemed ridiculous to me, too.

"What the hell were you thinking, man? Don't you know there are, like, a *million* fully-stocked gun stores that nobody pays attention to anymore? You can literally just stroll in the front door and help yourself. *Way* better self defense than an old farmer's poker. But don't worry, I've built up my arsenal pretty good now. You can use my stuff."

"Okay," I said. We were quiet a moment and I took a sip of coffee. It was nearly finished, and too tasty to have just one cup. I hoped there was more where this came from. "What's your name?" I asked.

"Arya. Good to meet ya." She clapped me on the back like an old buddy, then stuck out her left hand. "What's yours?"

I told her mine and shook her hand, then asked, "Have you ever come across any... others? Like us, I mean. Non-users."

Arya let out an exaggerated breath, a *puh-shooo* sound. "Not for, God... at least three years, probably more. Used to run into one here and there, you know? Before you really had to *hide* from them. I'd always try to get non-users to 'team up' with me. Join the rebellion, so to speak. Some did, for a little while. But eventually, everybody caved."

"Yeah..." I said, knowing all too well what she meant.

"Once, I captured one of them—a young girl—and brought her back here to see if I could sorta... *sweat* The Shot out of her system. She was thirteen, maybe fourteen, so I was able to catch her pretty easily. She was wandering around in a field, far off from any of the others, twirling a flower in her fingers and singing made-up songs about the Mothership. Fucked up how they get 'em young, isn't it? I snuck up behind her and put her to sleep with a mild sedative. Had to stick her in the neck with a needle from behind. Ironic, right? Anyway, I dragged her back here and tied her arms and legs down to the bed. Then..."

Arya paused and bit her lip.

"Then things got pretty bad. At first the girl would go through phases of sleeping for hours and hours, sometimes entire days, sweating and panting, breathing too quickly. Like that girl in *The Exorcist*. But then she'd be wide awake, her eyes all bugged-out, thrashing against her bonds and ranting all the Mothership bullshit. I tried talking with her, reasoning with her, but she wouldn't let me get a word in. Even tied to my bed, she was pleading with me to take The Shot, to 'open my eyes' and 'see the gift of light' and all that. She looked *horrible*, so pale and slick with constant sweat, like a white plastic mannequin covered in grease. And her eyes, so *empty*.

"She would yell and call out to me all through the night, shouting until her voice went hoarse. I got so sick of hearing her go on and on that I would sleep with earplugs in, two rooms away, and I could *still* hear her through the walls. It was like she had *endless* energy to keep talking and talking, and I mean, this was like *five* days after I caught her. The Shot was pushing her body further than it should physically have been able to go. I think that shit is practically *living*. It made a puppet out of her. She might not have been able to stop if she wanted to. I tried to give her soup and water, but she threw it all back up, and *that* scared me worse than anything. Users used to be able to eat regular food in the first couple of years, you know? Now I think something has been permanently altered in their biological make-up so that The Shot is all their body will accept anymore."

That conclusion might have seemed like a stretch to me at one time, but it made sense when she said it. Whatever was going on with users' bodies, they sure had not needed to eat or drink anything in years.

Arya went on.

"After ten days, the girl had made absolutely no change other than getting sickly thin. I felt like a monster, or a torturer, keeping her held down like that, but I knew to let her loose would be suicide. She hadn't eaten, hadn't gone to the bathroom, and was more concerned with convincing me to take The Shot than she was about being tied down. She slept a ton, like eighteen hours a day, and when she was awake, she yelled. I was baffled, I thought *surely* that shit would have cleared out of her by then, or that she ought to be starving for real food, but I think I knew in the back of my mind that by that point she was beyond saving. Still, I tried to hold out a little longer.

"Things got worse on the eleventh day. She started convulsing and writhing on the bed, straining her thin muscles to wrestle against the ropes holding down her limbs, arching her back and making terrible screeching sounds. Under her arms and legs were raw purple bedsores, and she was giving herself bright red rope burns. As a last ditch effort, I tried giving her water again or to inject her with antibiotics, but she gnashed her teeth at me and wouldn't let me anywhere near her.

"After three more days of that, I couldn't take any more. She was skeletal thin, just bones covered in skin wearing clothes that no longer fit her, yet somehow she still had the strength to fight against the ropes and scream. The last day, I stood there in the room, just watching her, dazed and kind of fascinated in a terrible way. I started to weep and scream back at her because I was so sick of it, sick of feeling like a torturer, sick of her endless screaming, sick of sharing a house with the half-dead shell of a person. It was horrific to watch her degrade like that, a little girl who had a life once. I was *pleading* with her to let me help, to not struggle, but she was completely *gone*. Whatever she had once been had been wiped clean by The Shot. To keep her like that any longer seemed more cruel than... well, than what I did."

Arya paused for a long time and stared at the floor.

"I put a pillow over her face and shot her in the head. I was crying so hard and shaking so badly I could barely steady the handgun. One huge bang, and her kicking went still immediately. It wasn't like killing the others. It wasn't anonymous with her. I... I didn't know what else to do, you know? I was just trying to help her, to force The Shot *out* of her body and make her a person again, but then... everything just got so *fucked up*."

"Holy shit," I said, quietly.

We sat in silence for a moment and I finished off my coffee, which had dropped to room temperature.
"Thanks for this," I said, setting the Garfield cup on the nightstand. "Haven't had any in a *long* time. Cleared my head up, I think. Glory and hallelu—"

I clapped a hand over my mouth.

"What. The. Hell," I mumbled through my hand. "I didn't mean to say that last part, it just came out."

"That'll happen," Arya said. "The Shot isn't clear of your bloodstream, and not quite out of your brain either. It'll wear off, you've only used it once. You were talking some in your sleep, too. Not a lot, but I think I heard, 'the island of Patmos,' and, 'I see one like a son of man, with hair like white wool and eyes like fire, and he rides upon a black horse.'"

"You remember all that?" I asked.

"Not the first time I've heard it. From the Bible, right?"

"Close, but they've—*I*, I guess—got it all mixed up, just like everything else the users say."

We were quiet again. I blinked hard a few times and looked around the simple room, shutting my eyes tightly and popping them open again. My vision was returning; things were clearing up and becoming sharp.

"Arya, where are we?" I asked.

"It's a condo on the top floor—the fourteenth floor—of an abandoned high-rise development on the edge of downtown. I've got the whole building to myself. Found this place about three years ago."

I recalled my narrow escape from the third floor of my apartment building, and had a sudden sinking sensation at the thought of being trapped. "Fourteenth floor, huh?" I asked. "You know, if the users ever found out you were in here, you'd be cornered. *Done for.* This high up, there's nowhere to go."

Arya grinned like she was way ahead of me. "Oh, I've got the place pretty well rigged to prevent that sort of thing. I've got all the ground floor entrances locked up tight and piled high on the inside with sandbags. They're *glass* doors which isn't ideal—not much I can do about that—but the barricade would sure slow anybody down that tried to get in for quite a while. The only door not sand-bagged is the rear service entrance that leads into the emergency stairwell. It's metal, not glass, has a steel deadbolt, and I've got the only key. Apart from that, I've got battery-powered motion detectors set throughout the lobby and first floor that will notify me immediately if anyone gets in. It's not as good as a security cam, but without power, it's the best I've got."

I nodded, impressed. "Clever work."

"The main elevators are permanently out of commission—again, no power—but I modified a smaller laundry elevator to be operated by a hand-crank pulley system. It's a bit of a workout, but it's better than hiking up fourteen flights of stairs every time I come home. That's how I got you up here, by the way. It would have taken forever to haul your passed-out ass up those stairs. Anyway, the users wouldn't think to look for the laundry elevator, so their only option would be the fire escape stairwells, which I've got booby-trapped with violent delights from floor one to fourteen. So if any users come sniffing around my building and actually manage to break in as far as the stairs, they'd be incinerated by an acutely-aimed blowtorch, stuck with enough animal tranquilizer darts to take down a pack of African elephants, or blown to smithereens by a cornucopia of military-issue hand-grenades with their pins rigged to trip-wires, and *that's* only up to floor three. If anybody got in, there'd be a shit-ton of death and destruction that would give me plenty of warning to fly the coop."

Arya folded her arms exaggeratedly and beamed at me, clearly impressed with herself in a way that I found endearing (and cute) instead of irritating.

"Floor thirteen is special, right below us." Arya pointed

to the floor. "I cleared the whole thing out, emptied all the rooms of furniture and stuff, and rigged it *to the tits* with chain-reacting explosives. Anybody who opens the door onto floor thirteen from the stairwell is gonna get a face-full of fuckin' fireballs. Absolute annihilation. Seems fitting, you know?"

I looked at her blankly.

"Thirteen. The unluckiest number."

"Ah, of course," I chuckled without humor. "But, if the floor right beneath us is full of explosives, if it was set off wouldn't it probably take out *this* floor too? Like, blast through the floors and maybe even bring the whole building down?"

Arya laughed brightly, but didn't answer my question.

"Um. Well, you mentioned time enough to 'fly the coop.' This high up, how would you get out if there was an attack?" I asked.

"A parachute."

She said this so matter-of-factly, I thought she was joking.

"Wait... Damn, you're *serious*, aren't you?"

"Of course! What a badass way to bail out of a burning building, right? Like a fuckin' Schwarzenegger movie come to life! Part of me has always hoped it would happen. Eventually it probably will."

I let out a small laugh. I couldn't disagree with her.

*

I staggered into Arya's bathroom—my motor functions had not yet fully recovered from the tranquilizers and hours of sleep—to take a shower from a hot water system Arya had designed herself that involved a propane heater and a five gallon glass carboy. It didn't take long for me to realize that Arya was extremely inventive and clever. The water pressure was low but the hot water felt incredible. It was the first real shower I had taken since the water companies shut down three years prior.

After the shower, I met Arya in the kitchen, which was lit with candles and battery-powered camping lanterns hung from the ceiling like miniature chandeliers. She had made us a veritable feast from canned foods: green beans, beef and vegetable stew, and sweet peach slices, as well as a bottle of red wine. I was used to eating canned food cold and wouldn't have minded if it was served to me that way, but Arya had a plentiful stock of propane tanks and had warmed everything until it swirled with steam from the plate. Seeing the hot, prepared food presented with actual plates and cutlery gave me a strange sense of Deja vu; a practice so distant from my experience I had nearly forgotten people ever ate dinner this way at all. It was as close to a luxurious meal as you could get, times as they were.

"Wow," I said, gaping at the dining table. "It's like... we're *humans* or something."

"And you even get to eat it, not just look," Arya said. "Grab a seat, dude."

I did, and told her, "Thanks, Arya. This is amazing."

"Don't get mushy. All I did was the modern day equivalent of warming up shit food in the microwave, only it took longer. Not exactly whipping up fine cuisine over here."

Arya sat on the other side of the table and used a corkscrew to pop the cork out of the wine. She poured hers first, not into a long-stemmed wine glass but a pint glass with a faded graphic that said "Budweiser: King of Beers." She filled the old beer glass almost to the brim, then handed me the bottle. The glass in front of me said "Shiner Bock" and featured a yellow ram's head. I served myself a pour as generous as Arya's.

We ate in silence; I, like a starved man and she, like a dignified person. I wolfed down a hearty serving of everything and helped myself to another. It was awkward, and I wanted desperately to talk with Arya—it seemed crazy not to take advantage of every second now that I had another sane human to talk to—but I was so out of practice with conversation that my mind was coming up blank. Having nowhere else to start, I began with a subject that I knew we would both be familiar with: The Shot.

"Have any theories on what The Shot *is*?" I asked. It was a stupid question and it came out clunky.

Arya took a deep breath. "I've had a few over the years," she said. "Like maybe that it was some weird sort of super-food. But manufactured by whom? And why so mysterious? So that didn't really make sense. Then I thought maybe it was an ultra-addictive pharmaceutical, maybe even tied to some big government conspiracy for mind control or to make everybody too zonked-out to know what the hell was going on. But, seeing as how we don't *have* a government anymore..." She chuckled without humor.

I had considered those things too, or versions of them.

"Or maybe it's nuclear runoff that bubbled up out of the ground that some idiot passerby found and decided to have a taste. Did you ever see that stupid old horror movie *The Stuff*?"

I shook my head.

"Yeah, it was crap anyway. Had some good gross-out moments though. Except in that one it was a meteorite, not nuclear runoff, and the stuff everybody gets addicted to looks like marshmallow cream."

Arya was quiet and seemed to zone out for a minute, staring at her glass and rotating it on the table. Then she said, "But none of those scenarios seem quite *right*, do they? The effects are too extreme. How could a drug of *any* kind cause the exact same experience in so many people? *Why* all the Bible shit, specifically? *Why* 'The Mothership' and the trippy space-talk? I mean, I've believed in some government conspiracies before, but I don't think even the brightest labcoats could stew up something that programmed everybody's brain the same exact way. And even if so, *why the hell* would it be in the form of a green fuckin' toothpaste that you shoot into your stomach? Plus, even if that was their plan, it must've backfired pretty hard since all of them are obviously using now, too."

I nodded.

"This sounds a little, uh..." she paused and shrugged. "*Crazy* is what I was going to say, but fuck it. What if the Mothership *is* the real deal?"

I stared at her and said nothing. She stared back, dead serious. I don't think I had ever let my mind consciously wander to the realm of seriously considering The Mothership as something real.

And yet, *of course* I had considered it, deep in the black corners of my subconscious, but had hoped the thought would eventually suffocate and die on its own. Arya was right; it *did* seem too crazy, too *out there*. But hearing her say it out loud seemed to validate something within my own head. It made it sound possible.

"I'm not sure how," Arya continued, "like, how The Shot got here or how there's a never-ending supply of it, or how people even figured out to start shooting it in their stomachs, but still... I don't think the shit is from Earth.

"Maybe one of... *them*—whoever *them* is—came to earth disguised as a human and started giving it out, showing people how to use it. An alien on the streets of Southern California, where it was first being used, probably wouldn't exactly be out of place. Or maybe they used mind control on a bunch of CEOs and government assholes, and provided the ingredients to manufacture The Shot in secret?"

Arya sighed and plopped her hands into her lap. "No, that's fucking stupid. None of that seems right."

She was quiet for a long time, staring at her plate. Then she gulped off the rest of her wine in a few long swallows. "It's all so ridiculous, like a bad sci-fi movie. One they would make fun of on *Mystery Science Theater 3000*."

"Our *lives* are like a sci-fi movie lately," I said. "No scenario is too far-fetched anymore."

We were quiet again. Arya poured herself another full glass of wine, the bottle nearing empty now. I felt unsure of what to say, being so long out of practice with human conversation. Arya was a talker when she got going, and at least we had our circumstances in common, but past that I was coming up dry for what to say. I caught myself getting nervous, clamming up.

Finally, I came up with something half-assed.

"So, you've got guns and grenades and other weapons," I said, listing the things off on my fingers. "And you've got water and propane and food..."

Arya nodded.

"You've got a place to stay that has proven to be pretty secure, for now, and we've got... well, we've got *each other* now." I felt my face flush red there and coughed into my hand. "Meaning we are most likely the only non-users for miles and miles, maybe the only non-users left *at all*..."

She nodded again, wearing an inquisitive look. Probably wondering where the hell I was going with all this.

"So... *what now?*"

Arya smirked, then shrugged again.

"The fuck if I know," she said.

*

Arya and I became quick friends, and I cannot tell if it was just a proximity thing or if we would have gotten along in "regular" life. Either way, it was glorious to have steady human company again.

She walked me through her vast domain on the fourteenth floor, which was made up of eight condominiums of about a thousand square feet each; four units on either side of a long hallway with double elevator doors at one end and an exit leading to the stairwell on the other. Skulls and crossbones had been spray-painted crudely in red on three of the apartment doors.

"This," Arya said, rapping her knuckles on one of the skull doors, "is my pride and joy, and the product of many hours of hunting and gathering. These three rooms make up my *arsenal.*" She said the last word with a growl, smiling in such a way that showed all of her teeth. "Or, as I like to call it, my Weapons of Ass Destruction."

"*Three rooms* full of weapons?" I asked.

"Yes, indeed!"

Arya beamed like a proud parent and flung open the first door. She clicked on a battery-powered lantern that hung from the ceiling and presented the room. "Just over 3,000 square feet of shotguns, handguns, semi- and *fully-*

automatic assault rifles, a few rocket launchers, cratefuls of rockets, a flamethrower, grenades of both the gas and exploding variety, baseball bats wrapped with razor-wire, and even a couple of fuckin' *Kill Bill*-status samurai swords. Probably not of Hattori Hanzo quality, though. Figure I could send off at least a couple thousand motherfuckers to their blessed spaceship afterlives with all this shit."

I laughed, sincerely impressed. "This is quite the collection. I don't even *recognize* some of this stuff."

She picked up an AK-47 and patted the barrel affectionately. "You know, I wish gasoline was still around. Then I'd find a Humvee too and fix it up. Keep it parked out front. I would trick *the shit* out of that fucker—full standing machine gun turret, a big old rack of high beam lamps across the front, maybe even rig up a rocket mounted to the chassis that I could fire from a button on the dash, *everything*. I'm talkin' *Twisted Metal* kill power, here. Then I'd go *hunting* for the Bible-babbling bastards."

"You're pretty resolved to this kill-first method with the users, aren't you?"

"It's either that or become one of them, man! You think they'd hesitate for even one second to stick you with the green shit under any circumstance? *Hell* no. So, in a way, it boils down to kill or be killed. Kill or be zonked out of your mind, more like."

"Yeah, I suppose so."

Arya popped the clip out of the AK and examined it. It was full to the brim of shiny brass rounds. She squinted with one eye into the clip housing, blew into it once, then slammed the clip back home with a satisfying click.

"Anyway, feel free to play around with any of this stuff," she said. "Chances are, opportunity will arise to use it before too long, so you may as well get comfortable with the equipment. Just keep in mind, I keep everything loaded and ready for action. Don't shoot your foot off or anything." She grinned.

I surveyed the room, nodding.

"You know, I *have* always wanted to use a flamethrower."

Arya smiled huge and clapped me on the shoulder twice.

"Attaboy," she said. "Strap it on and we'll take it outside."

*

Every evening after the sun had gone down, Arya and I would climb to the roof of her building and observe our lightless surroundings, dim grey in the absence of streetlights or lit buildings. There were no stars or moon visible; the sky had been blanketed with angry folds of wooly grey for several months by this point, and behind the dense canopy of clouds was an uncomfortable red and purple haze, like a congealed wound bleeding through a dirty wrap of gauze.

Arya would sling a sniper rifle with an enormous scope over her shoulder and hike it up the stairs every time we went to the roof. She insisted I also bring along a green metal box full of ammo. It was not long into my stay with Arya that I noticed she would never go outdoors without *some* firearm on her person, and usually several. She had even equipped me with a handgun on a hip-holster and an extra magazine that was to stay in the rear pocket of my jeans at all times. On the roof, we would scan the streets on every side through binoculars equipped with night-vision. And every night, we found the same thing: absolutely nothing. Always nothing. No movement, no users, certainly no *non*-users. Nothing but empty buildings, dead cars sitting at wild angles on rotting rubber tires, and streets overgrown with mammoth weeds bursting through ugly cracks in the pavement. Day or night, the world immediately outside our apartment was perpetually lifeless (or at least that is what the users wanted us to think).

Most nights, after our brief look-out expedition to the roof, we would stay up late in Arya's living room under the battery-powered camping lanterns and share a bottle of scotch or whiskey. We found that we shared an affinity for Jameson in particular. The only inventory that rivaled Arya's gun collection was her cabinet stocked to the nines with fine liquors, another product the users had long since abandoned.

And yes, we made love (if you could call it that), and have made love nearly every night—sometimes multiple times a night—almost since the beginning of my stay with her. It only took us about three days to get to the point of recognizing that we both wanted it badly and we dove headfirst into one frantic session that was over in under five minutes. What began as something animalistic and desperate (I mean, it had been more than four years for either of us; what can I say?) turned into something resembling true companionship and affection. We both understood that we might each be the last person the other ever knows in this life, so we figured we had better live it up while we can, with a future so uncertain.

*

From what we can tell, the users hardly ever go outside anymore, and when they do, they travel in packs with a sole purpose: hunting the unredeemed. These groups act as scouts—like the unfriendly bunch I ran into at the convenience store—to comb the landscape for non-users, although I cannot imagine that there are many of us left anymore. The users must have recognized at some point that it was easier for twenty or thirty of them to swallow up a lone non-user inside a crowd and force-feed The Shot to the poor soul than the old method of impassioned preaching to persuade the unconvinced. I think by now they have done all the persuading they are going to do, so it's on to Phase Two: conversion by force.

The rest of the users that are not out on soul-hunting trips stay indoors at their massive "temples" for howling Shot-fueled communal worship with arms and faces pointed to the heavens. They outgrew actual church buildings and synagogues long ago, so instead they meet for church in the structures that hold the most people; whatever places they can cram the most of themselves into. Their places of worship are converted sports stadiums, multiplexes, event centers, warehouses, and manufacturing plants that produce nothing anymore but the shouted praises of the enlightened, deep crying out to deep. It is not so much that Arya and I know these gatherings exist because we have seen them with our own eyes, but because we can *hear* them, even from miles away.

One night, their voices were especially loud as they sang some endless, formless hymn of insanity.

"Come, yes, come O Mo-thership. COME! Tarry not, Sweet Mo-ther, come nigh and lift us high, yes, LIFT US! Carry us all away to enter your hea-venly gates!"

Miles away from the nearest congregation (so far as we

knew), still the chants were loud enough to keep us wide awake, staring at the ceiling.

Eventually, Arya slapped her hands over her face and rubbed them downward, stretching out the skin below her eye sockets. She groaned, "Ah fu-u-uck, *shut up* already! When will those shitheads understand there's no ship coming for them? I'd like to hunt down their little shindig and personally *put a sock in it* for each one of them, and by a sock I mean a military-grade grenade."

I laughed.

She didn't, and became quiet for a long time. At last, she said, "How is this our *life*, man? It doesn't even seem real anymore, like we're not supposed to still be here."

"How do you mean?" I asked.

"Like, how can this be right? In what universe is this scenario seriously happening? What is the point of us still having our conscious minds if this is going to be the state of the world from now on? Hiding and scrounging and staying holed up in this goddamn apartment until they finally find us and shoot us up with the green crazy? I mean, shit, I'm glad you're here with me and everything—*really* glad—but is this how we finish out our lives? Just grow old in here and hope we don't run out of food and blast a few fuckin' users every chance we get?"

I did not know the answers to those questions since I had the same ones myself. But I wasn't sure she was looking for a solution so much as just a chance to vent, so I kept quiet.

She sat up in bed and went on, "I mean, Jesus, what if *we're* the ones who're wrong? What if The Shot, eerie and insane as it is, actually is the answer to unity for the human race or the end of the world or whatever? What if some E.T.-looking motherfuckers are up there in a flying tin can, just waiting for every last human being to give in and take The Shot and join the funny farm? Then once everybody on earth has been switched over, *then* maybe whatever comes next will... *come next?*"

"That's quite a theory," I said, quietly.

"I don't *want* that to be true, and most of me doesn't think that it is, but what else then? What's the alternative? *This shit?*"

I sighed and furrowed my brow, my stare burrowing into the ceiling. Arya had a point, and the implications were not pleasant to think about.

"I... I wish I knew, Arya. I really do. But I don't. And you're right, none of it makes any sense."

She bit her lip, and I could see glistening hints of tears welling beneath her eyes.

"Sometimes I just want to give in and take The Shot because I want to stop *thinking* so much. To stop caring about all the questions and utter madness, and just let the wondering be over. At least on The Shot, you're oblivious and happy, it seems, even if your personality and consciousness have flown the fuckin' coop."

We were silent, but the room was not; warbled, far off voices still sang through the walls.

"We are worthy, O Mo-ther! Let us drink from your ho-ly cup of gladness, let us be baptized in blood and raised to new, to new, TO NEW life!"

Arya burst out laughing in the darkness, and all at once I knew she was back. Relieved, I joined in, and we writhed in bed, clutching our stomachs and laughing our heads off at the ludicrous song bleeding through our walls from the outside. We howled until my ab muscles ached, and Arya wiped away laughter-induced tears with her palms.

"Ah, you know what? What am I saying? Every time

I think about just saying 'fuck it' and giving in, the users remind just how much I *don't* want to be one of them. I mean, can you imagine *me* down there along with them, singing hymns and crazy-ass songs with 900 stanzas, swooning around waiting for some spaceship to come take me off to la-la land? Or *you?* Can you picture yourself down there in like a fuckin' robe with a candle in your hands, shouting Kumbaya to The Great Space-Mom?"

We both chuckled at that, although most of the momentum had gone out of our laughter.

"You're right, I cannot picture that at all," I said. "I guess we're just not cut out to be users."

Arya sighed happily. "Ah, how could I forget? I just love blasting those bastards away too much to ever become one of them. Maybe the point of being alive now, in this world, is that we get to pretty much experience the lives of video game characters in a first-person shooter. It's like we live inside *Doom.* Did you ever play those games?"

"Oh yeah. *Heretic*, *Quake*, *Wolfenstein*, all of them. We even have the red and purple sky that looks all wrong, like on the *Doom* maps when you go outside, you know?"

"Hell on earth, man. Hell on earth. The monsters in our world just happen to look like people, and they can't throw fireballs yet, at least not to our knowledge."

We laid there for a moment, quiet again. The users were not.

"Shit," Arya said, and folded her arms behind her head. "What I wouldn't give to have electricity again and play a little *Knee-Deep in the Dead* on Godmode…"

*

I have been with Arya for six months now, which we have lived out in relative peace and comfort, considering times as they are. In another couple of months, we will enter into Year Seven since The Shot—approximately, since we don't know the exact date it showed up—and something definitely feels different lately. The air feels different, but I can't say how. There is the faintest whisper of an odd scent in the breeze for which my brain cannot find a category. My guts feel off, and while I have not gotten sick, I feel as if I could at any moment. It is an obscure, abstract, barely-there feeling, like an ominous presence behind a dark curtain that may be lying in wait to lunge, or may not be there at all. And I have no means to pull back that curtain and let the light in.

When we watch the users from our rooftop perch, they look like ants bustling in droves in and out of giant hills, more active than ever. Large numbers of them are coming outdoors now—incredible numbers, more than we thought was possible—whereas a few months back we didn't see any out at all. I suppose that when almost all of humanity is using the same drug and keeping themselves holed up inside stadiums and other massive venues, Arya and I cognitively *knew* that there had to be tons of them around, but actually *seeing* the monumental crowds of users pulsing through the streets provides a whole new perspective.

I have come to understand just how completely outnumbered we are and I think Arya has too, although we cannot quite seem to mention that fact to each other out loud.

We have gone out for short scouting expeditions, heavily armed, and monitored the users' activity with binoculars from atop various skyscrapers and high points in the city, and while they are still several miles away from reaching our apartment, there is no denying that they are on the move in our direction. They travel as one pulsing entity, smashed all together and consuming the space between buildings for several city blocks, like the Israelites might have looked shoulder-to-shoulder between the walls of the parted Red Sea. Part of what they're doing, we think, is combing every inch of the landscape for the last scraps of humanity that are not converted users. Droves of them will systematically spill into buildings, (*every* building, without exception—they're being quite thorough), and while we cannot see what they do inside, we can only assume that they are scoping out every floor, every office, every bedroom, bathroom, janitor's closet, and stairwell for any last non-user who might be hiding out in those places. It's the only explanation that makes sense; they wouldn't be looking for food, shelter, or clothing. Their only need any longer is The Shot. Their only pursuit, the dwindling lost souls who have not yet given into it. Their mission field grows increasingly small; the harvest that was once plentiful is now scarce.

Oh yes—one other *small* detail—once they have "cleared" a building, they set fire to it and move on. No good leaving a perfectly good building available to a future non-user to reside in. This makes for an increasingly charred and pock-marked landscape of black, smoking ruins; behemoths of steel and glass reduced to ashes and jagged heaps. With the dark red sky above and the flames below, all the world seems to be burning.

At night, the users return indoors to their tremendous structures for twilight worship sessions which last until morning.

We have understood for weeks that the users' destruction is moving in our direction—not quickly, but steadily enough to be worrisome. The dawning truth is that we have far too much stuff up on our fourteenth floor and not enough time to transfer all of it to another location, and even if we did, eventually the users would find *that* place as well and set fire to it just the same. The alternative is staying put until the users have burned a path to our front door, then we surprise them with a firepower shitstorm of biblical proportions. While it's an exciting idea, and I am confident we could send at least a few thousand of them off to Hades, I am also confident that we would eventually exhaust our ammo and be overtaken. There's just *so damn many* of them...

Arya, convinced of her own action-hero invincibility, does not share my concerns (or at least she pretends not to).

"Send 'em all after me, man. Open the goddamn floodgates," she has said. "I've got enough firepower to blast them all to fucking *Tim-buk-too*. We could even make a few more ammo runs while they're busy with their pyro-rampage and make a *serious* stockpile." (As if Arya's arsenal was not currently *serious* enough). "Any user thinks he's burning down *my* building has another thing coming, and I'll give you a hint: that *thing's* got a full-metal jacket."

I have to smile at her confidence, even if it is irrational and downright crazy. But under the surface, I'm not smiling, because it's that very confidence that might get us both killed.

ONE

We are both in a deep sleep when a thunderclap of praise jolts us wide awake in the full dark.

Arya flings the blankets off and leaps out of bed. The battery-clock beside us reads 4:37 a.m. She goes to the window and yanks aside the curtains, revealing the dead-black outside. The booming noise comes again. Voices, shouting.

"THANK YOU, MOTHER! WE HAVE FOUND THEM! PRAISE YOUR GLORIOUS NAME!"

"*Shit*," Arya says through gritted teeth. "*Get up!* They're fuckin' *here!*" she yells at me, shaking my feet under the covers as she passes the bed. I watch her bolt out of our bedroom and out the front door to the hallway, headed for the artillery rooms.

"This isn't right! How did they find us already? They never come out at night!" I yell after her.

"I guess *now* they fuckin' do," she calls back. "Now get your ass up and *gear up*. It's game time, this is the real deal."

I go to the window and peer down. My heart plummets, and suddenly I feel nauseated and weak. In the dim early morning light, I can see nothing but the dark figures of huddled users and their blank, empty faces, pointed straight at our window. The ground is not even visible between their bodies. They are crammed tightly together, surrounding the condo and filling the landscape of streets beyond in every direction for as far as I can see.

This is way too damn many of them.

We're dead, I think. The thought comes to me easily.

Flatly, without emotion. It's just a bald-faced fact, nothing more.

But no, not yet. Not yet, we aren't.

I jump when the users suddenly call out again.

"PRAISE BE TO THE MOST HIGH," they shout in unison. The volume of their cries is deafening. How do they all know to say the same thing at once?

"YOU HAVE DELIVERED THEM INTO OUR HANDS, O MOTHER, THAT WE MIGHT SOONER SEE THY FACE!"

A beeping goes off in another room—the motion sensors detecting something in the lobby—then another, and another, until the apartment is filled with the high-pitched bleating of the motion alarms. I guess Arya's sandbags against the entrance doors didn't last long after all, not with thousands of people pushing in on them at once.

"They are IN-SIDE!" I scream to Arya.

"No shit, Sherlock!" she yells back.

I throw on pants and a shirt and run through the living room, ears covered against the blaring chirps bleating all around. I run out the door and almost collide with Arya in the hallway.

She is already fully-rigged: an X crosses her chest, made up of one diagonal strap fitted snugly with dozens of gleaming brass rounds with pointed tips, each one as big around as my finger, and the opposite strap featuring a collection of plump green grenades. Two handguns are slung low on her hips, and an AK-47 hangs across her back. She has a rocket launcher hefted over one shoulder, loaded with a menacing red projectile. She is wearing only the high-cut pink pajama shorts and the faded black *Reservoir Dogs* T-shirt that she wears to bed, but covering her feet are rugged black boots— the same she wore on the day she rescued me—as well as a black headband and two black greasepaint smears, one across each cheek. And she's… *grinning*.

I can't help but just gaze at her for a beat, even with the blaring alarms behind me and the users probably already making their way up the stairs.

"Damn," I say. "Hopefully we live through this, because that is *definitely* the sexiest you've ever looked."

"Yeah, yeah," Arya shrugs, slyly. "I'm one Rambo-ass bitch, mother*fucker*," she says, and laughs wickedly.

With her hand that is not supporting the rocket launcher, she pulls me in at the nape of the neck for a firm, passionate kiss. Some of the black greasepaint smudges onto my cheeks.

"Now let's send some fucking users to where they've been begging to go," she says.

From one of the ammo rooms, I pick up the flamethrower because it seems like the right choice, and sling the full tank of fuel over my shoulders like a backpack. I also hang a double-barrel shotgun over my free arm and grab a big box of shells with brass ends and green plastic casings.

I join Arya in the apartment at the far end of the hall from ours. It's a sizable room, and devoid of furniture—Arya had cleared it out years ago, before I knew her—which gives us a nice, big, open space to run from window to window and have plenty of angles from which to shoot. Arya blasts open one large window with one of her pistols and scrapes off the remaining shards of glass around the edges with a crowbar.

I come to her side in the window frame and cock my shotgun. She winks at me and readies the rocket launcher on her shoulder. Then, shoulder-to-shoulder and with fiery eyes, we lean out the window and begin to rain down our judgment on all those who believe.

Arya screams a wild battle cry as she points the rocket launcher into the crowd and fires. Her body is momentarily knocked backwards and she stumbles a few steps into the room, but stays on her feet. Arya's shot produces a massive back blast of white heat that sears the carpet and wall behind us. Neither of us expected it, and I wince as a scorching hot pain hits me in the shoulders and back, but the heat recedes quickly. Arya grits her teeth and sucks in a breath, but shakes it off and returns to the window to watch the rocket. I am amazed at how silently the projectile sails down into the fading night, its burning red tail leaving a pluming trail of white smoke, as well as a ghost of glowing orange across my vision. The booming explosion that follows is enormous, and a splash of golden fire and seared body parts mushrooms out of the epicenter of the blast, lighting up the sky with a yellow flash.

Arya and I just stand there looking out the window, observing the beauty that her first shot created. It had to have taken out at least fifty of them, and injured two dozen more. In the aftermath, all that remains in the spot that she hit is a campfire of charred clothes and red corpses with ugly black scabs. The users watch this carnage unfold with a sort of blank unconcern. Then they turn their faces back towards us and howl with rage in unison—a throat-ripping, eardrum-bursting, inhuman scream—before they advance on our building with a new fervor.

Even in the low light from the fire, I can see their eyes glint and flicker with violent intention. I realize they are no longer interested in giving us The Shot; now they just want blood.

Arya tosses the rocket launcher down on the carpet and prepares another round. I lean my shotgun against the wall next to the window and grab the handle of the flamethrower, then lean out the window and point the ignited tip straight down. I squeeze the trigger and unleash a steady stream of flame which I guide back and forth parallel to the building. My hope was to create a rough perimeter of fire along the wall, but then I notice the thrower's flame sputtering out before it reaches the ground and I recall just how high up we are.

"Shit," I say, more to myself than to Arya. "We're too high up, I should have thought of that."

Arya says nothing, preoccupied with reloading the launcher.

Struck with an idea, I unhook the flamethrower's fuel tank from my back and rest it on the carpet. I point the still-lit nozzle out the window, its tiny blue-orange flame licking up from the end of the barrel. The fuel tank has shoulder straps like a backpack, and dangling below these are adjustable canvas strips. Carefully, I wrap one of these loose ends of canvas around the trigger of the flamethrower and secure it into a knot, locking the handle into a permanent firing position. A great jet of fire shoots straight outward from the window, horizontally into the sky as I hold the barrel level.

Satisfied, I point the flame down towards the users again and tip the whole apparatus, tank and all, out the window. The tank tumbles heavily through the air, dragging the whipping tail of flame along with it and casting wild streams of fire outward at insane angles.

The tank lands with an ugly thunk on some bastard's head who is up against the building, crumpling him into a human accordion. The spray of fire continues, scorching users point blank, engulfing the crowd in flames. There are so many of them smashed in together that the fire quickly catches on their clothes and bodies, igniting their hair and searing their skin.

I watch as the inferno grows to become an undulating pile of burning bodies lining the building wall. I hear squealing, screaming, and wet popping sounds. The users who are not on fire flop themselves on top of those that are, doing their damnedest to extinguish the flames. There is only one entrance door on this side of the building, and the users are shoving their way inside, some of them still partly on fire.

"Damn. I would have thought that would make a better barricade, they're still getting inside! Throw me your AK," I call to Arya, who is kneeling behind me fiddling with the rocket launcher, slapping and cursing at it.

"Come and fuckin' grab it off me then, dude! My hands are kinda full right now," Arya growls, slamming her hand down on the rocket, trying to click it into place. "Motherfucker won't *sit right!*"

I crouch behind Arya to unclip the AK-47 from where it is slung across her back. I feel her warmth as my hands undo the strap, and I can't help but want to touch her more, to hold her for a moment, to have a few more peaceful minutes alone together. Adrenaline is streaming through me, and even in the midst of chaos and very possible death, all I can think about is how gorgeous she is right now. And how I want to keep living if only to keep being with her.

Another thought comes, childish in its stupid simplicity: I don't want to die, I want to live. Plain as that.

Arya senses me delaying behind her, and whips her head around to look at me. Her expression is fierce at first, but then sees the look on my face and smiles, and I know that she feels the same warmth for me as I do her. The badass-action-hero part of her melts away for a second and she's just Arya, the tough-but-sweet girl with whom I've spent the past seven months.

"Better focus, you big idiot," Arya says, grinning. "Kill me some users and I'll fuck your brains out later."

I chuckle and feel an incredible anticipatory tingle zing through my system; shivers and a pleasant thrum runs through my nerves. Then I hear a heavy click and know Arya has gotten the rocket seated correctly in the launcher.

"Finally!" she says.

With the AK free, I return to the window and empty the clip in a rapid spray of bullets directly in front of the door where the users are still piling in. A score of them crumple and fall, creating a mound of bodies that will at least temporarily delay them from getting inside. Except I know that a handful—maybe quite a few—have made their way in already. They'll be coming up the stairwell to our floor soon. Hopefully, Arya's booby-traps, as well as deadly floor thirteen, will prove effective.

While users are heaving dead bodies away from the entrance, I yank the pin out of a grenade and let it drop into their midst. It sails down easily, like a balled-up pair of socks falling into a hamper, and lands right on target, creating a small pocket of death and making the mound of gore and bodies in front of the door even greater.

"Good work," Arya says, peering down. "Better go around and do that to the other entrances too. Hold 'em off, at least for a little. Every bit will help."

I nod and run out of the room with the AK plus two more magazines in hand while Arya steadies the launcher out the window for another blast. Before she pulls the trigger, she yells a well-known line from the *Die Hard* movies, cackling wildly.

The boom from the second rocket is muffled and distant, but I smile when it connects.

I am headed down the hall to the opposite side of our floor when, passing one of the ammo rooms, something bulky, black, and menacing catches my eye: an enormous machine gun leaning in the corner, four feet long at least and featuring double hand-grips of fat steel. The barrel is like a long cylindrical squirrel-cage of heavy black pipes. A brassy chain of ammo snakes from the gun's middle down to the floor and back up into a rectangular hole cut in the side of a wooden crate next to it.

I know shit-all about guns, but I do know that this thing looks badass. And *powerful.* It would be a downright shame to let such a beautiful beast just sit there unused.

I sling the AK around one shoulder and hang it from my back, then put one magazine in each back pocket to free up my hands. I grip the giant machine gun and attempt to hoist it up from the carpet floor—*good lord,* is it heavy. I lift it maybe a foot, straining and gritting my teeth, veins bulging and face probably bright red as a lobster, then stagger unevenly on my legs and slam the gun back down to the floor. The wooden crate nearby that houses the chain-length of ammo rests on bulky steel casters and sits about three feet high. I maneuver the crate (also damn heavy) towards the corner, then manage to heave the gun on top of it, laying it out horizontally for a kind of makeshift mounting table.

I wheel the rig out into the hallway and head for the large window at the end of the hall. From behind me, I hear a nearly constant *pap-pap-pap-pap-pap!* from the many rounds Arya is unleashing on the users below.

I push the crate until it slams up against the wall directly beneath the hall window. Luckily, the gun now sits roughly level with the windowsill. I whip the AK on its sling around to my front and take out the window in a quick burst of shots. The glass shatters into bright tinkling shards, raining down to the crowd below.

Outside, some shallow hint of morning light has begun to tease the sky; still that ugly purple and red glow. It's no sunrise—there hasn't truly been one of those for ages—but the new light, however weak, is welcome nonetheless. I look down to find (no surprise) that the users cover the ground and streets beyond in a tight pack on this side of the building, too. Shoulder-to-shoulder for blocks and blocks, maybe miles, and milling slowly into our building.

This ought to terrify me, but for the moment it seems far off, disconnected. As if some other person's home is being invaded by an incalculable number of drug-addled religious maniacs keen on killing the unsaved so that their savior ship will come. Instead, I feel a strange, emotionless calm, as if I were answering a business-related email that was only mildly important.

Heh, *email*. That used to be a thing.

Before I fire up the machine gun and pummel this side of the users' attack with rapid-firing lead, I decide to check the emergency stairwell to my left, as presumably some of them are already making their way up. Gun at the ready, I push open the door to the corridor. It is pitch black, I cannot even see past the first step in the first set of stairs.

On the rare occasions that Arya and I use the stairwell, we carry a battery-powered lantern to safely navigate through and around her many booby-traps. But without a light source, the stairwell (a windowless, rectangular concrete hollow with a fourteen story drop in its center) is as black as the heart of a cave; a suffocating, claustrophobic kind of darkness.

I sprint back to our condo and grab several military-grade high intensity glowsticks still in their black plastic wrappers from Arya's stash. She has probably close to 200 of them crammed in a bottom dresser drawer. I tear open the stiff packaging with my teeth, then twist and crack three of the glowsticks and shake them into illumination. Down the hall, I still hear Arya's continual rain of gunfire, with only short silent pauses in between. Reloading, no doubt. During those pauses, faint but distinct, I hear the distant, random cries of dying users.

Cautiously, I open the stairwell door and shuffle towards the center handrail with the lit green glowsticks held high in my left hand and the AK snugly in my right. I'm keeping light pressure on the trigger with my index finger. The sticks dully illuminate the concrete walls in a ghostly green haze, and while I see no users in my immediate vicinity, I *hear* their sounds echoing up the chamber. There is a sound of... *moaning*, guttural and agonized, from far below me. It's not just one voice, but several.

Arya's traps, I think. I didn't know what all these traps entailed, but some of the users must have already walked right into them.

Beneath the pained moans reverberating up the cavity was a softer, scratching sound; a sort of shuffle-and-clump, like an inelegant walk with only one functioning leg. Then it came again.

Sh-h-huff. Clump. Ssshh-h-uff. Clump.

One of them is still making their way up the stairs, I think. Maybe more than one, but it sounds like they're wounded. And slow.

I inch forward and hold the glowsticks directly over the center opening between the handrails that run back and forth in a blocky spiral all the way to the bottom. I drop one, then the second, the third, and watch them illuminate each floor in a quick green flash as they slice down through the air.

It occurs to me what a stupid move this was since it tells me exactly *nothing* about what is below. My visibility from this high angle is useless.

The glowsticks fall for what seems like a very long time, then slap the concrete on the ground floor and bounce to a stop, creating a tiny circle of soft green light.

Suddenly, at the bottom of the stairs, a heavy metal door bangs open with a screech—the exit door on the ground floor, forced inward from the outside. A flood of many voices rolls up to me, echoing off of the concrete walls. I hear a crowd of bodies bumping against each other and a great many sets of feet clomping steadily up the flights of stairs. I can see nothing, but the sound continues, and becomes greater.

Fuck. That'll be the rest of them, then.

I recede back into the hallway and slam the exit door shut. It has a spring-loaded horizontal metal push-bar in the center—installed on the *stairwell* side, of course—so I have no way of barring the handle closed or locking it from my side in the hallway. I shove the wooden crate serving as my gun mount in front of the door and kick down the wheel-locks on the casters. It's heavy, and will serve as a decent temporary obstacle, but if the users are already breaking through glass doors and sandbags then they'll be able to heave this door open easily and budge the crate aside.

I hear a muffled *boom* from deep in the stairwell, then a sharp, pattering clang of metal shrapnel hitting concrete. Next are high-pitched screams—not angry but *hurt* screams—echoing up the stairwell.

And, do I smell... smoke? Burning clothes, maybe. Or singed hair.

"They are *in the stairwell!*" I yell down the hall to Arya. "And gaining floors! I think the traps are only taking out a few at a time, there's a shitload of them inside now."

She does not respond at first, and I hear the sound of her unloading magazine after magazine.

During a pause, she shouts, "*They won't make it past thirteen, I gauran-fuckin-tee it!*"

A low growl emits from me over which I do not entirely have control.

"God *damn* it," I whisper.

Now Arya's overconfidence is annoying, because what if the users *do* make it past thirteen? What if something is rigged incorrectly down there and the explosives don't discharge? What if the users stroll right on past floor thirteen with zero interruptions and bust through the door directly next to *me*? What if thirteen is way overloaded with bombs and it takes out *this* floor too, blowing us all to holy hell?

Wouldn't even need any Mothership to come down and get us, I think. We'd be thrown up so far into the damn sky we could meet her halfway.

I am thrilled about none of these scenarios, then I realize that I can do absolutely nothing about any of them. Except... to lean this big-ass machine gun out the window and kill some users. That, and hopefully keep the stairwell door blocked for a little longer.

Say, and don't forget to try and stay alive *a little longer.*

Yeah. That too.

I hoist the machine gun off the crate and rest it on the open windowsill. An unexpected flash of memory reminds me why this gun looks so familiar. In an old movie from way before The Shot called *The Matrix*, the main character, Neo, used a gun just like this one—except his was attached to the side of a helicopter—to blast through a bunch of windows on a skyscraper and rescue his friend from the computer-agent guys. Neo is wearing all black and sunglasses that were considered cool in the 90's, and while he is obliterating all these huge windows into miserable tiny shards of glass, there are brassy bullet casings and pieces of seared shrapnel raining down like hot confetti from the gun barrel to the streets in slow-motion. It has been a long, long time since I've seen that movie, but that scene has always stuck with me because it's beautifully shot, epic in scope, and makes one feel hyped up, like a badass.

Well, now is my opportunity to *be* the badass.

I tip the heavy barrel out the window and angle it as low as I can without risking it leaning too far and ripping right out of my hands. The gun features no sight (anyone using this big fucker shouldn't need to *aim*), but I squint down the length of the barrel anyway to see where I've got it aimed. In my line of sight is an undulating ocean of users for as far as I can see, churning and milling in fleshy waves ever closer to our building.

I focus the bulky, multi-barreled business end of the gun in that general direction and let it rip.

The barrel whirs into a spinning blur of metal as great flashes of light burst from the end, producing a rapid palpitation of bullets into the users below. The steady spray of bullets reminds me of some long-forgotten carnival game involving a water-pistol where the objective was to shoot down the "tongues" of fake wooden clowns with hideous faces. Whoever could fill up a water balloon underneath the clown and make it explode first would win a prize, usually some shitty China-made stuffed knockoff of a cartoon character.

The sound is incredible—*shockingly* loud—and I wince as my ears are instantly overwhelmed by the deafening bursts beating against my head. The individual rounds have become indiscernible trails of continuous yellow fire as they rocket themselves out of the chambers, one after the other, only milliseconds apart. Both of my arms are flexed against the pattering blasts, and my entire torso is jarred and rattled by the gun's intensity. And, like in the movie, shreds of scalding shrapnel spit out from the barrels; winks of hot golden metal flickering down to the ground.

I can only vaguely see the destruction that I am creating. With all the vibration and flash, it's hard to know exactly what is going on any further than the end of the spinning barrels. I can, however, perceive two encouraging things: the distant sound of screams, and the sight of blood bursting in my line of fire, squirting upward and outward like great globs of red paint. The rounds must bear an incredible amount of force, as even with the users' elevated, superhuman strength, it only takes one or two rounds to put them permanently out of commission. I could point the barrel almost anywhere and still be mowing down users at this point. They are tumbling over dead in wave-like patterns; wisps of wheat being tossed around and blown over by a heavy wind.

Some obscure corner of my mind wonders what Arya is up to, and part of me wishes that she was with me, next to me, seeing me in action right now; a user-killer after her own heart.

The users scream in rage and gnash their teeth at me from below, and attempt to throw bricks or rocks at the window in which I stand—as if these futile actions will do me any harm at fourteen stories above them. They are now beginning to hoist each other up on shoulders and make a human ladder to reach a window on the second story.

Those clever bastards.

They reach a second floor window and smash their way inside within minutes. More of them stream up the human ladder of users that remains firmly in place.

I cannot aim at these users because it would mean pointing the enormous barrel straight down and I would surely lose the whole apparatus under the weight. Instead, I continue to focus my remaining rounds on the users that I *can* hit, and hit many scores of them I do. Probably hundreds.

I create a nice wide semicircle of crumpled bodies on the ground arcing outward from my vantage point in the window, and the users still standing outside of this crescent give the whole scene the appearance of a human crop-circle, except that the fallen "stalks" are bloody and writhing. The approaching users now have to climb and stumble over a field of their dead companions in order to reach the building. That slows them down somewhat, but not enough.

My fingers, hands, and arms are numb from the constant shimmying of the gun. I realize that I am in desperate need of a break soon, lest I lose all feeling in my hands and let the gun fall from my grip out the window.

Only then does an extremely obvious fact occur to me: the chain of ammo railing out of the crate is not infinite, and at some point those rounds *will* run out.

I look to the floor on my left only to watch the last brassy strip of rounds slither out of the crate, into the gun, and out the other side empty. The spent chain clanks to the carpet as the spinning cannon whirs to a stop within seconds. There are wisps of smoke rising out of each barrel. My ears are ringing with a sound like an old dial-tone and I hear a soft *clickclickclickclickclick* in the new silence. My finger is still jammed down on the trigger. I release it and let the gun balance on the sill.

Below, the users have continued to make their way up the walls and into the building with fervor. There are several human ladders now, allowing users entrance into multiple windows and balconies. The bodies of the users I slaughtered have been covered over by their surviving comrades swarming towards our building, and the horizon beyond is still thick with droves of more, more, more.

I *had* to have killed at least two or three hundred of them, but it hardly made a dent in their army; like stomping out a bunch of ants on the sidewalk and thinking you've killed them all, only to see their true numbers come pouring out of the anthill.

I just stand there for a moment, arms at my sides, looking down at the writhing mass of them, dazed, trying to focus my thoughts enough to contemplate a logical next move. We've got the stockpile of weapons, but—a new realization of blistering clarity—no possible hope of killing all of them. They are choking in on us *way* too fast. I think if an entire SWAT team armed to the teeth had a trained professional positioned at every window on every floor of this building, they would *still* have trouble keeping up with the flood of users coming at us.

It comes to this, then.

We are about to become users, I think. Converts at last.

They win, good game everybody. Handshakes and "attaboy" slaps on the ass all around.

These thoughts pass through me with surprisingly little emotion attached to them. I'm too numb, or too shocked, or too tired to care.

Maybe it won't be so bad. At least we won't know any different once they've plugged us with the green shit and The Shot has taken over all of our thinky-parts. Might even be pretty happy, actually, like Arya has said. Ignorant and blissful. Part of the new fam. The worldwide fam of bat-shit crazies.

I am lost in my thoughts, swaying on my feet, when

time slows down and three things happen at once.

One: the door to the emergency stairwell on my left bursts inward, sending the wooden crate blocking it skidding across the carpet and slamming into the far wall as a screeching crowd of bloody, injured, enraged users begin clambering into the hallway.

Two: the floor thrums and rumbles beneath me with such intensity that it feels as if the earth's foundation is angrily shaking itself apart.

There is a sensation of carpet and concrete warping and bulging under my feet like a wave, knocking me off-balance. Then comes the noise of an explosion so jarring and indignant it is as if sound itself has been broken, torn in half, and the blaring, *living* thing underneath has forced itself into the world through a staticky threshold that it was never meant to cross.

FLOOR-THIRTEEN-they've-gotten-into-FLOOR-THIRTEEN-and-set-off-the-damn-explosives-goddamnit-Arya-you've-killed-us-all-you've-killed-them-and-us-both-you-and-your-fucking-FLOOR-THIRTEEN.

Three: a hand slaps my shoulder, grips my shirt, and spins me around, nearly toppling me over on the uneven floor.

Arya. She is sweaty, smeared with black oily gunk, and bloody.

(*bloody-bloody-why-is-she-bloody?*)

My ears are sounding a high-pitched alarm in my head and have clapped their sensors temporarily OFF for protection against the audible assault around me. It feels as if cottonballs have been jammed into my ear canals, making every sound muffled and distant.

I can still lip-read the words Arya shouts in my face.

"*Move, motherfucker! To the roof, it's time to go!*"

She yanks me towards our apartment door as users flood the emergency exit behind us.

In the apartment, portions of the floor have bulged upward in bloated swells of torn carpet and concrete blown to chunks. Other sections have fallen through, exposing crumbled foundation and twisted rebar snarling in every direction. Licks of fire peek through the holes in the floor and singe the plastic seams of the ripped carpet, turning the openings a charred black. Smoke the color of sawdust is quickly filling our apartment.

Arya leads us through the living room which, apart from the fire, smoke, and the pack of wild users behind us, is its own pocket of chaos with the blaring chirps of dozens of motion alarms going off, each one blipping a red indicator light rapidly as if to say *LOOK AT ME, LOOK AT ME.*

"Watch your feet, keep to the walls!" Arya says. "Any part of the damn floor could be weak and dump us into the fucking inferno."

She is dragging me so fast and so closely behind her that I could not stray from her path if I wanted to.

We reach the bedroom and she slams the door shut and locks it. It's only one of those wimpy thumb-turn locks on the handle that can be undone from the other side with a hairpin, but it's better than nothing. The users probably aren't going to take the time to find a hairpin.

Arya flings open the door to the walk-in closet, shoves aside a slew of our clothes on their hangers, and crouches for a hefty army-green backpack leaning in one corner. She turns and hurls this pack into my midsection.

I catch it, but let out a *whuff!* from the unexpected impact.

"Strap that on, nice and tight," Arya says, and pulls on a pack of her own.

I sling on the pack and secure the buckles over my chest and stomach. It is *damn* heavy, thirty pounds or more. It's a wonder she was able to chuck it across the room at me.

"These are the parachutes?"

"Yeah. Hope you're not scared of heights. Come on."

I can tell she's trying to maintain her usual hard-ass demeanor, but her voice is trembling. Her hands are doing the same.

A wooden ladder is leaning against the back wall of the closet that was previously obscured by hanging clothes. Its rungs lead upward into a jagged black opening cut into the ceiling. I knew it was there—Arya had mentioned it before—but prior to this, I had never paid it much attention. Foolishly, I thought that we would probably never have to use it.

Without a word, Arya climbs the ladder and disappears up the hole. Chalky white pebbles of drywall crumble away from the roughly-cut edges and make a small mess on the floor.

I sigh, baffled that we are even doing this, that what is happening *is* happening, and follow her up the ladder.

Sounds of chaos and rumbling come from all around us, muffled and grating. The building groans from its cement and steel innards as if it is weary of standing, as if it might decide at any moment to just go ahead and let itself fall to pieces and swallow us all with it.

I pull the ladder up inside the hole and lay it aside to keep the users from coming after us. I can hear the bedroom door begin to snap and splinter inward as Arya and I disappear further into the darkness of the ceiling.

Arya knows her way and moves steadily on hands and knees through the dark network of obstacles in the ceiling. I shuffle clumsily behind her and try to keep up. It's tight in here, the roof is only about three feet above our heads. There are boxy aluminum channels of ventilation ducts to crawl under or over, as well as lengths of piping and tangles of wire beneath our hands to maneuver. I curse more than once, jamming my knee into an unseen copper valve or hitting my head on a metal vent.

This industrial maze we blindly navigate takes my thoughts away from our *larger* situation. I forget that we are crawling through the insulated guts of an apartment building fourteen stories in the air in an attempt to escape almost certain conversion and possible death at the hands of a mass crowd of insane, drug-riddled humans swarming through the floors beneath us.

We are not so different from kids, I think, goofing around in an abandoned building, pretending we are lab rats in a giant metal maze and making up a game that we had to find our way out in a certain amount of time or *THE SCIENTISTS IN THE WHITE LABCOATS WOULD GET US*. Except that the prize at the end of *that* game—the cheese, so to speak—would simply be getting to climb out of the abandoned building—safe, alive, unconcerned—with our friends when it got too dark outside, then go home for a warm dinner.

The complete darkness of the ceiling has an oddly cozy, familiar quality to it that reminds me of simpler, happier times. I want to lie down, curl into a fetal position, and just be still for a while. Stay here in the black cove of the ceiling and shut my eyes and breathe deeply and *rest*—finally rest— until the building burns down and I die in the flames and falling debris, or until the users find me and carry me off to wherever and make me one of them. Or until I open my eyes, wake up, and find all of this ridiculous shit done and gone, only a nightmare.

But then there's Arya.

She is reason enough to keep living, to keep moving, to see what happens next. So I follow the sound and scent of her through the dark.

I hear a scurrying, scratching sound behind us. The users are hoisting themselves up into the ceiling hole, meanwhile moaning their spiritual calls (yes, *still*) in a last-ditch effort to convert us. As if we would just decide right here and now, actively crawling away from them in the pitch-black after they destroyed our home, that *Oh sure, guys. You're right. I guess we'll finally take some Shot with you. Your tainted gospel sounds great after all.*

"Here it is," Arya says. She feels around above her head, then pounds upward with the side of her fist on what sounds like a thick, warbly aluminum panel.

We seem to be at the furthest corner of the building from the hole we came up through, best as I can figure.

Arya pounds harder and harder, the metal letting out warped twanging noises that resonate through the chamber in brief echoes.

"*Fucker's... STUCK!*" she huffs between punches.

Finally, the edges of the metal piece—a hatch that opens to the roof, I realize—budge upward with a screech and a dim outline of light shines through in a square shape. Another strike from Arya, and the metal square swings up on hinges, arcs in the air, then lands flat on its back with a crash. Cold air rushes in and hits my face, and the hideous red-purple-grey sky is now visible. Arya stands up in the opening and pulls herself onto the roof. I follow her and swing closed the hatch door behind me.

It is... quiet.

No, not completely.

There is a light wind brushing at our clothes, and a distant sort of murmuring coming from far below, but the users ceased their constant chanting. The building makes creaking, unhappy sounds beneath our feet; the groans of metal twisting, wooden joists bending beyond the limit of their strength, cinderblocks grating against one another.

Arya un-slings the shotgun that was strapped to her back and pumps a round into the chamber. Not much good it will do from way up here, but it is one of the only weapons left on her person. I have a pistol tucked in the back of my jeans and two magazines, but I leave them alone for now.

We look at each other. Arya's face is stern, but looks as if it will break at any moment. There is fear in her eyes, she isn't trying to hide it anymore. I feel as rough as she looks. I am scared, there's no way around it.

We approach the lip of the roof and peer down.

An inhuman roar tears through the sky and scrapes at our eardrums, the throaty chorus of a thousand angry saints; a million, myriads upon myriads of sinister angels, come to bring enlightenment and doom. The battle cries of every war movie I have ever seen do not come close to this. There is death in their shouts. A hymn of Hell.

The users have their arms outstretched to us from the ground, reaching, clawing—

(praising, giving thanks)

—roaring after us with great gaping maws full of spittle, red flesh, and too-white teeth.

We step back and Arya stares at me with flat, wide-eyed terror. Her body is trembling, every façade of toughness has fled from her. I can feel tears running down my face and my ears are ringing terribly, distorting my thoughts.

"We have to r-run," Arya manages, and wipes away tears from her cheek with a shirtsleeve. "We have to run like h-hell from one end of the roof t-to the other, and jump. Jump like you've never fucking jumped before. Jump like you're gonna just fly the hell right over all those bastards. Then count to five as you fall and y-yank the cord. That'll deploy the... it'll deploy your pa—"

Arya's face crumples into a grimace and she grits her teeth. She dips her head and weeps into her hands.

"*God damn it...*" she whispers. "God *damn it!* We... we've lasted so long, we were *so* careful, this wasn't supposed to happen! We were supposed to make it out of this bullshit *alive!*"

I pull her into a tight hug, as well as I can with the huge mound of the parachute pack strapped to her back, and she cries into my shoulder with her hands covering her face.

My heart is on overdrive inside my chest, as if trying to punch its way into the open air by slamming itself against my rib cage. My mind is sprinting for a solution, scrambling for a way out of this, but no idea presents itself. I am nauseated and unsteady on my feet as I hold Arya. I'm as scared shitless as she is, but she was supposed to be the strong one, our anchor, my refuge, the badass who always has an answer (or a bullet) for everything. Seeing her like this makes me feel as if the last frayed handle of reality to which I cling is about to be ripped free from my grasp.

Not ten paces behind us, the metal hatch we have just come out of bangs twice, then flings open with a crash. Users stand up in the opening, darting their heads around the roof, looking like the snakes that adorned Medusa's head. They spot us and begin streaming out of the hatch with outstretched hands.

There are ten, fifteen, twenty, more than thirty of them on the roof now, each with wide, white eyes and too-small pupils. The hot, rancid breath from their collective mouths hits us in a wave, even from several feet away, and their dry, grey tongues waggle as they recite their speech in unison in an appalling monotone.

"*Please, young brother and sister, enough with this denying of the sweetest fruit! 'Suffer the little ones to come unto me,' our Mother says, 'but if the children will not come, lay hands on them and BRING THEM TO ME.'*"

"Time to go," I say. I pull back from her hug and hold her at arm's length. "Time to jump, *now*."

Arya lifts her head and meets my eyes. Hers are tear-streaked and bloodshot, but her smug composure has returned. She looks to the users shuffling toward us, and sighs in mock-exasperation, which makes me smile.

"*God…* these fuckin' guys just *do not quit*, do they?" she says.

The users are feet away and closing, but Arya takes the time to pull me in by the nape of my neck for a rough kiss. She then unhooks a grenade from her belt, snicks out the pin with her teeth, and spits it onto the roof. She tosses the explosive underhand—gently, like you would a baseball to a little kid—into the belly of the nearest user.

Even in their brain-dead state, the users must still have reflexes, because this dumb fucker *catches* it. By the time he realizes what he's palming, we are sprinting towards the opposite edge of the roof.

Arya is ahead of me by a few strides. I run after her, and as we approach the edge of the building to fling ourselves off of it, I find that I am… *laughing*. Hysterical. Maniacally. Crazy as a loon, having the time of my life.

Arya reaches the edge of the roof, plants one booted foot on its lip, and gracefully launches herself into the air, knees tucked up to her chest with the shotgun pointed down between her legs. She seems to hang there in mid-air for a moment and float outward from the roof in slow motion, her clothes rippling in the wind like the undulating body of a jellyfish. I have my eyes fixed on the lip of the roof and am mentally readying myself for what I hope is an equally effective take-off.

Maybe, I think, we really *can* glide on our deployed chutes past the ocean of users, sailing just beyond the edge of their crowd (even though we can't see if there *is* an edge from our vantage point), landing on open ground in a sprint, ditching the packs, and running like hell to whatever safety we can find.

A fool's hope.

I reach the lip of the roof, bend my right knee to mount the edge, and shove myself upward and outward from the building. The shock of beginning to fall hits me immediately. The breath catches in my lungs, gets trapped there, and refuses to release. I hadn't been prepared for this, the stomach-dropping sensation of plummeting towards earth. Like a million dreams of falling off a cliff, except for real. There would be no jerking awake just before impact with the ground.

My limbs are flailing and I'm trying to convince my lungs to *breathe.* In my panic, I almost forget altogether where we are, what we are doing. Some distant corner of my brain registers Arya below and ahead of me, floating steadily down with her chute deployed.

My hands scramble for the parachute's rip-cord on my right shoulder. I find it, and yank it... but far too soon. I hear a ruffling sound behind me as the chute plumes open.

I am jerked roughly to a halt and get the wind knocked out of me. My limbs fling forward from the sudden halt of motion, like I'm a marionette dropped from a great height and yanked back to dangle on its strings. I feel my body swing backward, then I slam into the wall of the building.

Looking up, I see that my chute has snagged on something protruding from the building. Even though it felt like I had been falling for *minutes*, it could not have been more than three or five seconds. I deployed the chute way too early, and have fallen the length of only two or three floors from the top.

Idiot.

Fucking idiot.

Now what are you gonna do?

Looking down, my stomach does backflips at seeing my feet kicking over open air and the mob of users far below, reaching up for me. If the ropes that support the chute snap or the canvas tears loose, I'll break my back just from the fall, let alone the users getting at me.

I look out towards Arya and my heart sinks further.

She has already drifted almost to ground level and hasn't gone nearly far enough to clear the users. She's coming down right on top of them. The users are swirling and writhing and shouting beneath her, jumping up and snatching for her ankles.

Arya keeps her legs tucked up and begins firing straight down at them with the few rounds she has in the shotgun. Each blast takes out only two or three of them in pulpy wet splashes of red and grey matter. She empties the gun and hurls it down at them, then unhooks a grenade.

But it is useless.

A user gets hold of Arya's ankle and yanks her down into their midst.

I watch, helpless, dangling in mid-air from ten stories up as the users surround her on the ground. They swarm her, swamp her, overtake her completely. There is not a syringe of The Shot in sight.

No, they have different plans.

They hold Arya down on her back and pull up her shirt, exposing her stomach. Using their hands—their *bare*, wretched hands—they stiffen their fingers into claws and dig their fingernails into her stomach until they break the skin, then tear and peel back the flesh of her belly, opening a horrible, ugly red maw in her middle.

I weep and convulse and kick at the air, screaming her name over and over. Arya's eyes have rolled back and her body quivers. She is still very much alive. She seems to come in and out of consciousness, though I can only see her face between the users' bodies for seconds at a time. They begin to pull out her intestines and entrails. And with faces turned to me in hellish, knowing glee, they begin to eat her alive. Everything coming out of Arya is red and purple and terrible; from a nightmare. It seems unreal. Surely they cannot really be doing what I'm seeing, doing this to my Arya, to the strong woman who has killed so many of them, who saved *me* from them.

My screaming reaches a fever pitch and is no longer words, just screeches raking out of my throat. The hate inside me is dizzying, the pain I have for Arya feels like it will break my mind at any moment. I burn after the users, I want them dead, I want them all dead *now*. I want to be on the ground and rip them all to fucking pieces with my bare hands and eat their hearts raw, putting an end to their final pulsing beats with my teeth. I want to set them all on fire and watch them suffer and sizzle and die, *finally* die, and it feels like I am capable of all of these things in this moment, all of them and more.

I remember the pistol tucked in the back of my jeans. With the distance between us and the rage and tears blurring my vision, it takes me five shots to put a bullet in Arya's head and end her misery. I empty the rest of the magazine into the crowd at random, screaming, screaming, screaming for all of them to die. I taste blood in my throat and keep screaming. Still I scream as the users pull me up and back inside.

*

I am on my back on the carpeted floor of one of the apartments in our burning building where the users hoisted me up by my chute through a window. My shirt is pulled up from where they have just given me The Shot. They don't have me tied up or bound in any way. No point now. They have not killed me, and I know why.

They *wanted* me to watch Arya suffer, to see the light go from her eyes, and for me to live with the pain of having seen it for the few remaining moments I have left before my mind turns and I am gone.

But you know, somehow, I know that things will turn out all right because *glory, it will not be long now bef*—no, no, *SHUT UP!*

I pound at my temples with my fists.

That's not you, that's not you.

Fight it. FIGHT. IT.

God, it's already happening.

The room is crammed full of users, and I lie in an open circle on the floor that they've made around me. They are all watching me, grinning their vile, inhuman grins. Eagerly awaiting my transformation.

I know I should want to scream at them, hate them, kill them, but the rage is slipping away from me. The indescribable fury inside me for what just happened to Arya is softening, my body relaxing, my mind easing into tranquility under a cool bed of *clouds, just as we will rise to meet Her in the clouds of the air with the greatest trumpet shouts! Come, O Moth—*

AAAAYYURRG, GOD DAMN IT, NO! NO NO NO! Shutup-shutup-shutup...

I curl into a fetal position and claw at my head, moaning and howling, but also fighting to concentrate with all I have to HOLD. ON. TO. *ME.*

My brain. *My* thoughts. Truth, reality.

I can keep those things if I just fight the shit pulsing through my body. I've had it in me once before, and I beat it then.

Yeah with Arya's help, idiot. No one's gonna be nursing you with tranquilizers here.

I can *will* myself not to change. It's only in my head, a souped-up hallucinogen. It's only mental, after all, and it can be *overcome, just as I have overcome all enemies and loosed all binds! The death of Death has come and you will join Me in glory—*

I dry heave and twist on the floor, clutching my middle and uttering low, guttural retching sounds. I flex every muscle in my body, my face burning and dripping sweat. I am physically and mentally *wrestling* the substance that is invading my consciousness.

But The Shot's plea inside me is too strong. The visions and ideas it presents me with are too... *wonderful* not to behold.

The users begin to sing something over me, and their voices are angelic, beautiful. It sounds like a hymn.

A brother takes my hand firmly in his and helps me to my feet on the carpet. Suddenly, all feels well with my soul, with the world, with the universe. Outside the apartment window: *stars*, like outer space. Whole planetary systems, entire galaxies. Right there, within my reach. It's the most beautiful, incredible sight I've ever seen.

And I'm going to go *there. To live in it, forever.*

With tears in my eyes, I embrace the brother closest to me, and the room fills with the sound of clapping and cheers.

My voice trembles with utmost joy as I tell them that I have tasted, I have finally seen.

ZERO

In the end, it was not one ship that came, but many.

The red and purple darkening of the skies marked the ships' presence long before they revealed themselves for the purging. Just beyond the grey canopy of clouds, they had already arrived and were spread across the globe, hovering low in the atmosphere, carefully observing.

The beings aboard the ships watched as the events played out beautifully, and on schedule, for a number of years. However, they became impatient when their deadline drew near and a mere few—several dozen out of the billions on Earth—kept themselves hidden and would not partake of the gift that the beings had so graciously offered. In the final days, the whereabouts of these hesitant few were set upon the hearts of the worshipers, revealed like a whisper. The rebellious were then dredged out of their hiding places and into the open. Conversions were made by force.

Seven years unfolded, to the very day, from the first convert to the last (though no human party ever ascertained this precise timing), until every living, breathing soul on the face of the earth had been changed, and made new.

It was only then that the ships descended together in grid-shaped patterns, spread out like nets over the occupied areas of the planet, dipping just below the surface of the clouds and finally into view. Their dark and discus-like forms hung in the air for a time, silent and still.

The worshipers gathered in the streets and cheered as one people, one united race, celebrating the long-awaited arrival of that for which they had hoped. They sang and danced with joyful tears in their eyes, and embraced one another in gladness. Salvation, it seemed, had finally come. They called out to the ships in unison, asking to be raised up, to meet their Blessed Mother in the air.

The hulking ships remained stone-like and quiet, hovering in place.

The users grew in fervor and shouted even louder. *Surely we are not being heard*, they thought. *We must impress The Mother with our praise!* They flailed and convulsed their bodies in a mad dance, vying for the attention of the fleet. They screamed and sang and wailed with flapping tongues, waving their hands and jumping up and down to be seen.

Still, the ships remained unchanged.

The worshipers became worried that they had done some wrong, or were deemed unworthy to be saved, so they cried out in anguish, pleading not to have to wait any longer to be lifted to paradise. They bellowed and shrieked until their throats were hoarse. They began to weep aloud with hands on their heads. Their cries rang out across the landscape, the sound of their moans carried high into the heavens. Great floods of tears were shed.

Perhaps a sacrifice, they thought. *They will see the red of our blood and know that we are faithful.*

Knives and pencils and broken shards of plate or pot and razors and jagged hunks of concrete and wooden stakes and pieces of bone and wedges of broken glass and twisted aluminum and sharp stones and branches and thorn-bristles and teeth were used to tear open the wrists or chests or arms or feet or stomachs or genitals or thighs or scalps or breasts or shoulders or heels or tongues of the worshipers in Shanghai, in Mexico City, in Dehli, in Chicago, in Tokyo, in Lagos, in Moscow, in Houston, in London, in Manhattan, in Singapore, in Sacramento, in Montreal.

Again a great flood was shed, but of crimson.

High over the worshipers' heads, light pulsed awake in the sky as each vessel displayed a glowing blue ring set into its dark form.

A renewed shout of gladness rumbled out from the worshipers, despite their choked and weary throats, despite their many and varied flesh wounds. At last, their time had come.

The azure blue rings of the vessels began to rotate in unison while the ships remained still. They spun slowly, but with increasing speed, until they were thrumming circles of blurred blue. The intensity of the revolutions began to shimmy the ships in their places, giving them the appearance of pulsing rapidly against the clouds. A low groaning that was felt more than heard reverberated through the atmosphere.

The ground began to shiver and quake beneath the worshipers' feet and tiny pulses hummed up through their bodies as if they were tuning forks of flesh. Excitement began to build anew as they prepared to be lifted into the air and carried to their perfect home in the sky.

The ships shuddered furiously in the atmosphere as the blue rings pulsed at incredible speed, and the warbling bass-note emitting from them only grew in ferocity.

The worshipers cheered and waved their arms, even those that bled openly. *Any moment now*, they thought. *Surely at any moment, our feet will rise up off the ground, and we will be weightless and free! Oh, yes, Mother, make it so!*

Blue rings spun impossibly fast. Vibration boomed down.

A worshiper clutched his stomach in the midst of the crowd and bent double, his mouth yawning open in a horrified O, as if preparing to retch. Animal-like grunts and squeals choked out of his throat—strained and hideous sounds—and the veins on his neck and forehead bulged green and ugly purple against the slapped-red color of his face. His eyes bulged and were bloodshot. Spittle sprayed from his pink lips, and sweat ran from his face in a trickle. His expression was one of unadulterated terror.

Throughout the crowd came scattered shrieks. They backed away from the man and watched his struggle in fascinated dread, the thrumming ships above momentarily forgotten.

The worshiper's stomach glowed suddenly like an orange ember beneath his shirt. The fabric caught fire as his belly began to burn from the inside out. A ring of red and yellow sparks expanded in his middle, dissolving away the flesh there as flames licked out from where his organs ought to be. His lower back began to glow and burn as well, just above his buttocks, until a fiery hole had opened there too.

Worshipers all around him screamed and backed away, others only watched in disbelief.

Within moments, the small blaze had eaten away his intestines before they had a chance to spill out onto the ground. His spine, charred black, was now visible between his top and bottom halves, as the flames had completely consumed his abdomen. His skin and tissue dissolved upward and downward at once; a pulpy-wet apple core chewed out in the center. The white-hot embers plumed through his chest and down his legs, disintegrating the meat from his bones until every tendon and muscle and cluster of fat had sizzled away into greasy smoke and nothingness.

At last, the flames ingested the worshiper's shoulders, neck, and head, quieting whatever gagged sounds he was still able to make. A smoking, ash-black skeleton was all that remained. It collapsed to the ground in a tinkling clutter of charred bones.

Worshipers turned and fled, shoving against each other in mass chaos, trampling those they had previously called brother or sister, clawing their way to an escape that would not be found.

Within moments, they, too, bent double, retching and clutching their stomachs.

Strangled sounds rippled through the multitude as one after another bent over—ten at once, a hundred, a thousand, then millions—uttering choked howls and pressing their stomachs. Some fell sideways to the ground and curled into a fetal position, moaning and rocking themselves, begging for the heat to stop. Others held their middle with one hand and raised the other skyward, crying out for relief, for rescue.

Before long, not a one was left standing erect.

Overhead, the ships thrummed furiously with spinning blue light.

Almost at once, seven billion roses of white-hot heat bloomed inside the soft bellies of every worshiper on the planet. The searing petals ate their way out through the tender flesh of the worshipers' stomachs and proceeded to combust into oblivion what was once called the human race. Great was the inferno that poured out from myriad bodies that day. Greater still, their cries of anguish.

Heaps and mounds of smoldering black bones covered the surface of the earth with wisps of white smoke rising off of them. Flecks of ash and sparks danced on the windless air, and the greasy, bitter smell of burnt meat hung over all in a grey haze.

The whole of the event began and was completed in the span of seven minutes, perhaps ten. What followed was a silence on the earth so complete, so whole, that it rivaled only the dead, cold quiet of outer space.

The ships above brought their blue rings to a noiseless halt.

In the stillness, the fleet began to descend as one, lowering slowly from the heavens to the earth. Just before their hulking dark forms touched down on the landscape, hatches slid open soundlessly from the face of every ship's hull.

Inside each was movement, and glowing green light.

AFTERWORD

I must attribute the genesis of *The Shot* to two things.

First, a dream—or rather, a nightmare (the first of my stories to have sprouted from one, to my memory). In early 2013, my wife and I were watching a lot of *Parks and Recreation*, and while what I am about to describe sounds admittedly silly, it felt dead serious and vividly terrifying at the time. In this dream, I was outdoors on an open street in a big city, and a ways off from me were great crowds of people, bustling and talking. Amy Poehler and Rashida Jones (*I know...*) walked up to me from the crowd and began telling me very sternly that I needed to take something that they were simply calling "The Shot." Amy had a syringe at the ready in her right hand.

"Everything you see becomes something else," they kept telling me.

That phrase I remember most vividly of all, which is why it ended up a few times in the book. Amy and Rashida were speaking passionately about the wonderful effects of the drug. I told them I was not interested, but they became angry and insisted that I take The Shot with them. I began to back away, but they each put a hand on my shoulders and held me in place. The dream ended when Amy jammed the needle through my shirt and into my stomach.

Before I woke up, I *felt* the sting of the needle.

Echoes of that nightmare are all over this book, but even after having had such a specific dream, the idea for what would become *The Shot* had not yet fully materialized in my brain.

A few months later, I watched an endearingly bad little slice of B-movie horror called *The Stuff* (notice any similarity between my title and theirs? Nah, me neither). *The Stuff*, directed by Larry Cohen in 1985, is by no means a great movie, nor one I would even take the time to watch again, but its concept is an interesting one.

A meteorite crashes in the woods, breaks open, and white goop that looks like marshmallow cream comes bubbling up out of it. An old man stumbles upon the white stuff on the ground and decides to—why not?—scoop some up in his hand and start eating it. Turns out it's delicious, and the rest of the movie is about The Stuff becoming an extremely popular and heavily-advertised consumer product, packaged in ice cream-like tubs and eaten as such.

One of the best parts of the film is the extensive branding for The Stuff: radio jingles, jovial TV spots and bright, shameless kiosk advertisements in grocery stores. The only trouble is that The Stuff is addicting and eventually kills people in some colorful ways. The side-effects of The Stuff on humans are random and inconsistent (one of the film's major issues is that it doesn't make a lot of sense), but the death scenes make for some fun biological gore and special effects.

What I liked about the movie was the idea of something unknown becoming so universally popular and being widely consumed primarily because it was branded well, and that no one eating it bothers to investigate where it comes from or what it might do to their bodies or health. I also liked the ambiguous nature of The Stuff's origins, another concept I employed for *The Shot*.

To be clear, *The Stuff* and *The Shot* are two very different stories—watch the movie and you'll see what I mean. But

The Stuff provided a few creative puzzle pieces that had been missing from my idea for *The Shot* and helped me realize what kind of story I wanted it to be.

As for the book's Biblical content, to me, that stuff was just a distraction; a smoke-and-mirrors ploy implanted into the users' heads by way of The Shot to keep them from devising what end was truly coming to them. I also felt it was an interesting theme to explore from a writing standpoint. It is not a commentary on the Church universal, nor a satire of Christian faith, so any double-meaning you may have read into the text is purely unintentional. I was careful to make it abundantly clear that, one, the Scriptures used in the book were being wildly misquoted and taken out of context by the users, and two, those Scriptures were being spoken by people of very unsound mind. Lastly, I took care to not have the users say anything that was directly heretical against the person of Jesus Christ, nor His death on the cross. Blasphemy was not my goal here.

That said, the readers who found this book to be blasphemous probably hurled it into the fireplace and mourned their wasted dollars long before getting to this afterword and reading my true intentions. Oh well, those people are not the first readers I've lost (*The Pirate-Ghost of Hole 19* comes to mind), nor will they be the last.

Until next time: Taste, brothers. See, sisters. Keep watchful eye to the skies for lo, even so, The Mothership approaches.

-D.G.
Denver, CO
May 20, 2015

ACKNOWLEDGMENTS

I must first thank my wife Emmy for her ongoing encouragement and support throughout the writing of this book. As with *every* other project I have *ever* taken on, there were plenty of those nights when I could be found lying face-down in my pillow, whining about how I was no good at writing, about how the book would never get done, about how life is pointless and everything is terrible. Em was the one who put up with that garbage (and continues to), and who was always gracious enough to talk me down from hurling myself into the pit of despair. Life would be a lot uglier without her.

Secondly, I owe a great many thanks to Jonathan Raab who was willing to give this book a chance. His contributions helped whip my story into much better shape and bring clarity to the scattered manuscript I gave him. I've been working with Jon off and on for two years now, and I don't exaggerate when I say that his insight and fair criticisms have made me a better writer.

And lastly? Thanks to you, Dear Reader, for picking up this book. Heaven knows there's an ever-expanding plethora of things to read out there, not to mention the slew of other distractions in this world on which we choose to spend our time. Thanks for being willing to spend a few hours with me. I hope it was as much fun to read as it was for me to write.

Doctor Gaines is the author of a number of stories, including the novella *Clara's Quilt* and *Michigan, Ten Cents*. The latter is currently being adapted into a film, set for release in 2016. Doctor lives with his wife and daughter in Denver, Colorado. His work has appeared in *Spooklights* and *High Strange Horror*. He is an editor for and contributor to Muzzleland Press. *The Shot* is his first novel.

Subscribe to Doctor's email list for infrequent, non-spammy updates when he releases a new book and for access to free content exclusive to subscribers. Doctor blogs and reviews books at www.doctor-gaines.com. He tweets useless but occasionally entertaining things at @DoctorGaines.